"Marriages end every day," Josh said. "I should've known better in the first place."

"What do you mean?" Tasha asked. At one time he'd been quite romantic. Josh was the kind of man women loved to marry because he was a one-woman kind of guy who cherished the family. His bitterness caused sadness to spill over inside her for the boy who'd lost his belief in love.

"Forget it. It's nothing I want to talk about."

"I'm sorry," she said softly, knowing her words were inadequate.

"What's done is done," he said. Their eyes met again and Tasha wanted to look away for fear of catching something he had ___ ___ share, but she couldn't. Her ___ ___ she held his gaze, won ___ ___ to affect her after ___

Josh broke ___ ___ poke again, at least the s___ ___ everything happens for a ___

"That's what som___ ople believe."

"You don't?" he said, catching what she didn't say.

"No." She left it at that, and he didn't press.

Dear Reader,

There is a saying "Everything happens for a reason," but when something terrible befalls us, it's hard to remember that simple wisdom. Sometimes our pain blocks the message we were meant to receive but eventually we get a second chance to benefit from the experience.

Natasha's story is all about second chances in love and forgiveness. Sometimes it's easier to forgive others but hardest to forgive ourselves. Natasha faces this lesson head-on as her family hits a crisis and her return home places her in the path of the man she gave her heart to as a teen. Their reunion is bittersweet as both struggle with the feelings of self-doubt and fear that threaten the love they share.

This was not an easy story to write. At the time this book was written, my family was going through its own personal crisis and there were moments when the emotion coming from the page was merely a reflection of the turmoil of my own heart.

But this story was cathartic for me. Knowing Natasha had a happy ending gave me hope for my own.

Hearing from readers is one of the highlights of my day. Feel free to drop me a line anytime. You can write me at P.O. Box 2210, Oakdale, CA 95361, or at author@kimberlyvanmeter.com.

Happy reading!

Kimberly Van Meter

P.S. Look for Nora's story soon! She's fiery, ornery and obstinate—only a special kind of man could handle this woman.

RETURN TO
EMMETT'S MILL
Kimberly Van Meter

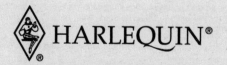

TORONTO • NEW YORK • LONDON
AMSTERDAM • PARIS • SYDNEY • HAMBURG
STOCKHOLM • ATHENS • TOKYO • MILAN • MADRID
PRAGUE • WARSAW • BUDAPEST • AUCKLAND

ISBN-13: 978-0-373-71469-8
ISBN-10:   0-373-71469-6

RETURN TO EMMETT'S MILL

This edition published by arrangement with Harlequin Books S.A.

® and TM are trademarks of the publisher. Trademarks indicated with
® are registered in the United States Patent and Trademark Office, the
Canadian Trade Marks Office and in other countries.

www.eHarlequin.com

Printed in U.S.A.

ABOUT THE AUTHOR

An avid reader since before she can remember, Kimberly Van Meter started her writing career at the age of sixteen when she finished her first novel, typing late nights and early mornings, on her mother's old portable typewriter. Although that first novel was nothing short of literary mud, with each successive piece of work her writing improved to the point of reaching that coveted published status.

A journalist (who during college swore she'd never write news), Kimberly has worked for both daily and weekly newspapers, covering multiple beats including education, health and crime, but she always dreamed of writing novels and someday saying goodbye to her nonfiction roots.

Born and raised in scenic Mariposa, California, Kimberly knows a thing or two about small towns—preferring the quiet, rural atmosphere to the hustle and bustle of a busy city any day—but she and her husband make their home in Oakdale, which represents a compromise between the two worlds. Kimberly and her husband, John, met and fell in love while filming a college production. He was the camera operator and she the lead actress. Her husband often jokes that he fell in love with his wife through the lens of a camera. A year later they were married and have been together ever since.

Books by Kimberly Van Meter

HARLEQUIN SUPERROMANCE
1391–THE TRUTH ABOUT FAMILY
1433–FATHER MATERIAL

To Krystina Morgainne for your gift of hope.

To Wynette Kimball for your expertise and wisdom during a time of great emotional upheaval.

To my children, Sebastian, Jaidyn and Eryleigh, for understanding when Mom was glued to her laptop.

To my husband, John, for his determination to continue growing, learning and loving together even when it's hard.

And finally, this book is dedicated to anyone who's ever had to face something painful in their past in order to embrace the future. Your courage is your strength and a gift to yourself and others. You deserve good things. Never let anyone convince you otherwise.

CHAPTER ONE

THE DRIZZLE FALLING FROM the gray skies blended with the steady drone of Father McDonald's voice until Tasha Simmons lost the ability to tell them apart.

The dull gleam of her mother's casket mirrored the gloom of the skies. Tears welled and receded until Tasha's eyes and throat ached.

Flanked by her sisters, Nora and Natalie, and Natalie's husband, Evan, she blocked out the pain that came with the knowledge her father was only one sister over, and she locked her knees to keep from sinking to the ground.

Suddenly, the short holiday visits over the years weren't enough. Not nearly enough to get her through something like this. She'd give anything to have one more day with her mother. Just one day.

Fingers tightening around the black plastic umbrella handle, Tasha blocked out faces she'd known her entire life until they were as anonymous as the raindrops pelting the small group. It seemed a lifetime ago that she'd ever been the girl they remembered.

The priest ended his reading from the scripture meant to offer some measure of solace to the ones left behind, and everyone murmured "Amen." He gestured to her father who, with Natalie's help, approached the casket with slow, stiff steps, a rose clutched in his hand. Tasha averted her eyes, not wanting to watch as her father disintegrated into harsh, shuddering sobs. Staring at the wet ground, the rain creating muddy rivulets down the side of the hill her mother would be buried in, she suddenly hated her sisters' decision not to cremate. Tasha didn't want her mother lowered into the cold ground, surrounded by worms, ants and other disgusting insect life. The grief she was holding back rose in her throat and she struggled to get a grip.

Her mother wasn't supposed to die so young. She wanted to scream it to the heavens until her voice was hoarse or until it disappeared entirely.

It wasn't supposed to end like this.

Father McDonald indicated it was their turn and the three of them placed their snow-white roses beside that of their father's. Bitterness filled her mouth and tainted her thoughts. What significance did placing flowers on a casket have on anything? Her mother could not enjoy their beauty or smell their sweet scent.

Tasha passed Nora as she returned to her place and startled at the red-rimmed stare she received. There was more than grief in her sister's slate eyes and there was no doubt in Tasha's mind that it was directed toward her.

An apology was useless; she wouldn't even try. Their mother was dead. Would it have mattered if she'd come home any sooner?

Father McDonald gave his final words, ending the short service. She dragged a deep breath into her lungs, then a shudder followed as the cold went straight to her bones. Tasha murmured to Natalie that she was leaving but was stopped by a hand on her shoulder.

"Tasha?"

"Hello…" She racked her brain for the woman's identity, but even as the woman drew closer, a sad smile on her plump face, Tasha's mind blanked.

"I'm so sorry about your mom. She was such an amazing woman."

Tasha nodded and dabbed at her eyes with the handkerchief clutched in her hand. The woman kept talking, and a spark of recognition flared in her mind, but Tasha couldn't remember her name.

"Goodness, what's it been? Fifteen years or so since you left home to go to Stanford? What were you studying?" The woman shook her finger at Tasha in thought. "No, don't tell me…anthropology! That's right. You were getting a degree in anthropology. How'd that work out for you?"

"Ah…well, I've been working for the Peace Corps," she offered, struggling to fan the spark into something less frustrating than just the fleeting image of a long-ago friendship.

"You don't remember me, do you?"

Tasha hesitated. She didn't want to hurt the woman's feelings when she'd clearly cared enough about Tasha's mom to attend the funeral, but there was no help for it. She shook her head regretfully, but the woman graciously waved away her consternation.

"Don't sweat it. I don't exactly look the same as I did in high school. Not many of us do, well, except you, of course. You don't look as if you've aged a day. Plop a tiara on your head and you'd be the spitting image of you at seventeen when you were prom queen."

A frightening thought. Tasha stiffened and searched out her sisters. Natalie caught her beseeching stare and hurried over as quickly as the cemetery mud and her shoes would allow.

"Hannah, how are you?" Natalie asked, a pleasant smile fixed to her face despite her obvious fatigue. "Things good down at the hardware store?"

Hannah Donner. Tasha slapped a mental hand to her forehead for blanking on someone who'd once been a close friend. It seemed unfathomable that she'd forget Hannah's name, but weariness and grief had robbed her of higher mental ability. Always the forgiving sort, Hannah seemed to move right past Tasha's momentary memory lapse and nodded in answer to Natalie's question, but her expression dimmed appropriately in light of the reasons they were gathered. She reached out a hand and Tasha reluctantly accepted. "I'll always remember your mom like she was when we were in high school—the cheer squad's very own personal team mom. Nobody made better brownies."

"Thank you," Tasha choked out as a wave of unwanted nostalgia clogged her throat. Memories of sleepovers, girl-talk, childish dreams and blissful sighs over cute guys rushed her brain as she struggled against the sensation that she couldn't breathe. She was relieved when Nora trudged up to them, her expression hard.

"Are you coming to the wake?"

Tasha averted her eyes, inwardly flinching at the anger in her youngest sister's unforgiving stare. "Uh, no, I'll probably just head back to the hotel for some rest," she answered, catching Hannah's nod of understanding and Nora's darkening frown. "I'm pretty tired—"

"I should've known." Nora cut her off and continued toward her vehicle with short, angry steps.

Tasha watched as Nora climbed into her truck and held her breath in alarm as her sister drove too fast out of the cemetery parking lot.

"She's taking this pretty hard, isn't she?" Hannah asked, though the question was rhetorical. Missy's death had taken a toll on the entire Simmons clan. Only Nora covered her grief with the anger she held against Tasha.

Natalie pressed her lips together as if to apologize for their youngest sister, but Tasha read understanding in her middle sister's eyes and felt outnumbered.

They were ganging up on her. And, the reason chafed.

A letter, written in Natalie's flowery script, appeared in her memory and she bit down on her bottom lip. She hadn't known. Couldn't have known. The original letter had somehow been eaten by the postal service, and by the time the second letter arrived a month later the cancer had moved with deadly accuracy throughout their mother's body before she could board a plane. Yet, her sisters blamed her.

"Tasha?"

Natalie's voice penetrated her thoughts and she realized both women were staring.

"Are you all right?" Hannah asked, taking in Tasha's rigid state.

Tasha slowly unclenched her fists and offered a small smile. "I'm tired," she answered, and Hannah nodded her understanding.

"Of course you are," she said. "After everything, I'm sure you're exhausted. "Well, uh, call me while you're still in town and we'll go to lunch. Catch up on old times."

Tasha nodded with false promise but shuddered privately. *No, thank you.* The past was a place she rarely visited.

And for good reason.

JOSH HALVORSEN WENDED his way through the departing crowd following the service, sadness at a vibrant life cut short dogging his steps. He hated the saying that God only took the good ones, because somehow it seemed a penalty for being a decent human being. Growing up, Missy Simmons had been like another mother to him, though at times, he certainly felt one had been enough. Ahead, he saw Tasha talking with Hannah Donner and his breath hitched in his chest as he saw her in the flesh after all these years.

He slowed his pace and people flowed around him. At one time they'd been inseparable, crazy in love until it had ended badly and he'd limped away nursing a broken heart and bruised ego.

The last time they spoke was the day they broke up during her first year at Stanford. They learned quickly long-distance relationships were hard to maintain—even when the love was strong. In the end, fear of losing her coupled with irrational jealousy eventually drove a wedge between them even their love couldn't withstand. The echo of their last words ghosted his mind and regret followed.

He'd thought time had dulled those feelings, but the moment his eyes alighted on her willowy figure, wrapped in an austere black woolen overcoat, he'd known by the startling zing that sent his heart racing that he was wrong.

An invisible connection flowed between them, tethering him to the spot despite his desire to blend into the crowd. He'd paid his respects, nothing more was required of him. Perhaps…but he couldn't bring himself to walk away as if he'd never been there. Good manners dictated he offer his condolences to Gerald Simmons…and to Tasha.

"Tasha…" Her name felt foreign on his lips, almost forgotten, but he knew that was impossible.

"Josh."

His name came out in an astonished husky murmur that reminded him of other times, and for a split second he wondered how things might've turned out if different choices had been made. He glanced away, shoving his near-frozen hands deep into his jacket pockets, until he could look at her without distraction.

"I'm sorry about your mom," he offered, his gut twisting at the pain he read in her red-rimmed green eyes before she concealed them behind dark glasses. "She was a good woman who didn't deserve to die so young."

"Yes, she was." Tasha nodded. "She thought the

world of you," she said, drawing a deep breath. "And she would've been happy to know you came."

"I'd heard she was sick. I was hoping for a recovery," he said, noting the subtle differences in Tasha, none being uncomplimentary. She was still beautiful. Maturity had treated her well, accentuating her natural grace and refining her soft, cultured voice.

"Thank you," she said, bringing her umbrella down closer to block out the wind that was wreaking havoc on her fine hair that hung loose to her shoulders, the moisture in the air bringing out the stubborn curl she used to hate. He remembered playing with the soft strands, twining them around his finger on lazy summer days spent down at the Merced River.

"You haven't changed a bit." The observation drifted out of his mouth and her startled yet instantly guarded reaction made him wish he'd kept it to himself. She gave him a brief smile that hovered too closely to patronizing to be taken at face value, and he sensed more had changed than he realized. "Take care, Tasha," he said, and quickly moved on.

He was nearly to his truck when he heard his name called. Turning, he was surprised to see Natalie hurrying toward him.

"The wake is at my parents' house. Please come," she said, once she caught her breath. "Mom loved you like a son. You are always welcome in our home." She hesitated, as if weighing her decision to continue, then added resolutely, "Tasha would like it, too."

Somehow he doubted that. "It's nice of you to offer, but—"

"But nothing. You were once friends. And, right now, we all need our friends. You know?" She finished with a smile that begged even though her words had not. Like Tasha, Natalie's eyes were red-rimmed and puffy, her nose pink from both the frigid weather and her tears. "Please?"

Against his better judgment, he nodded slowly and she exhaled as if in relief, her breath creating a gray plume of mist before them. "Then it's settled. You'll come. It'll be nice. For everyone."

With that she turned and joined Tasha, who was waiting in the new Honda sedan he assumed belonged to Natalie.

He knew the smart thing was not to go, but a part of him wanted to see her again. And that desire worried him. She was part of his past, not his future. That much he knew. But, as he climbed into his truck, his thoughts returned to the very place he didn't want to go.

She'd been the cutest girl on the cheer squad and he'd fallen hard. He missed those halcyon days when his biggest concern was passing Algebra II and beating the rival football team at Homecoming. Theirs had been a clichéd romance. The jock and the princess. But it'd been great while it lasted. Too bad he'd been too dumb to see what a good thing he'd had. He shook his head, annoyed at the maudlin direction his thoughts had taken, reminding himself that life was what he'd made of it.

A heavy sigh felt trapped in his chest. What the hell was he going to say to Tasha at the wake when it was obvious they'd said all they needed to say to each other years ago? He should've been firm, but he'd never been the kind of man to turn a woman down when tears—or even the hint of tears—were involved.

Besides, it was the least he could do for the family he'd once considered as his own.

CHAPTER TWO

TASHA SHIVERED DESPITE the warmth caused by too many bodies crammed into the small house of her childhood. Slipping out on the pretense of needing to help Natalie in the kitchen, she removed herself from the crush of people and wandered away from the family room.

If things had turned out differently, would she have stayed? Raised a family like Natalie? Started a business like Nora? Trailing her fingers along the wainscoting, she detoured to what used to be her room. The plan had been to turn it into a sewing room, but it still looked exactly as she'd left it. Sinking to the single bed, she inhaled the unique smell of a closed-off room and her gaze roamed the corkboard where dozens of postcards were pinned. A painful smile formed as Tasha envisioned her mom pinning a new one to the board after she'd read it.

"I thought you said you weren't coming."

Her sister's voice at her back made her wipe at the tears gathering at the corners of her eyes before she turned and answered. "I wasn't. Natalie persuaded me to change my mind," she admitted, watching warily as her sister came into the room. "It's good to see you, Nora," she added truthfully.

Nora softened a little. "You've been missed. It's been too long since you've been home."

Four years. The longest she'd ever been without making a short stop in Emmett's Mill.

"I know. I was stationed at a medical clinic in Punta Gorda and there just never seemed to be a good time to leave. They're always needing volunteers. I didn't want to leave them shorthanded." She avoided Nora's gathering frown, turning away with her arms wrapped around herself. "It isn't like I can just call up a replacement, Nora. There isn't even phone service in some areas. My job isn't like that of most people. I can't just leave. People need me."

"Your family needs you, too," Nora retorted, the anger returning to her voice. "*Mom* needed you."

She turned, tears pricking her eyes. "I know," she said, accepting the harsh look Nora sent her, knowing her anger came from a place of pain and grief.

She tried reaching out, but the burn coming from Nora's bloodshot eyes stopped her. Dropping her hand, she shrugged helplessly. "Nora, my being here wouldn't have stopped the cancer. She was going to die whether I was here or not."

"You're right. But maybe if you'd been here, the last name on her breath wouldn't have been *yours*." Tasha startled at the revelation and Nora stepped forward, her voice beginning to tremble with the force of her anger. "Maybe if you'd been here, she wouldn't have suffered through a broken heart, as well as the pain of the cancer as it ate her from the inside."

"Stop." Tasha closed her eyes, blocking out the tears coursing down her sister's cheeks. What could she say? Nothing would erase the fact that she had been thousands of miles away while their mother suffered through pancreatic cancer. She slowly opened her eyes again as the silence lengthened. Nothing she could say would convey how sorry she felt, so she remained silent.

Nora wiped at her tears and then pinned Tasha with a look ripe with bitterness and sorrow. "What can I say, Tasha? You simply should've been here."

"I *know*," she answered quietly, though there was an edge to her tone. She accepted Nora's condemnation…to a point. And that point had been reached. "You've said your piece, now let it go, Nora. You're not the only one grieving, you know. I lost my mother, too."

Nora's jaw hardened and Tasha wearily prepared for another stinging backlash from her youngest sister, but to her surprise it didn't come. Instead, Nora swallowed hard as if choking down whatever she'd been tempted to say next and gave Tasha a short nod. "I didn't mean to start a fight. But, the last few months have been hard. Really hard. And it would've been nice to have our eldest sister here with us. That's all." Tasha gave an almost imperceptible nod and Nora continued softly. "We needed more than postcards, Tasha. Paper is no substitute for flesh and blood."

Let it go, for pity's sake! Frustration swept through her as she stiffened against Nora's attempt at burying her under a mountain of guilt. Mission accomplished, little sister. A snap retort danced on her tongue, but she didn't want to spend the brief time she had before returning to Belize fighting. She began to offer a truce, but Natalie, who appeared in the doorway, looking fatigued and exasperated, cut her off.

"There you two are," Natalie broke in, peering

into the room with annoyance. "Nora, I could use your help with the hors d'oeuvres trays, and, Tasha, could you help me with the guests who just arrived?"

Suddenly sensing the tension in the room, her gaze darted from one sister to the other. "What's going on? Are you two fighting already?" She didn't give either a chance to answer. "No, I don't want to hear it. I need your help. Whatever squabbles you guys are having can just wait. Besides—" she sent a dark look to them both "—I'm sure you two can agree this is not the *time* or the *place* to be airing your dirty laundry."

Chastised, Nora left the room without an argument.

"At least she seems to listen to you," Tasha said with a weary sigh. "All she wants to do with me is argue."

Natalie considered this, then said, "Tasha…she doesn't really know you. You left when she was sixteen. All she knows is that you weren't here when you were needed. Her memory of you is shaped by the image she created when you weren't around."

"And now I'm here and the reality of who I am is a disappointment?"

Natalie rubbed at her eyes, the tiredness there pulling at Tasha's conscience. What was she doing? Natalie was right. Now was not the time. "Forget it.

I understand. Just point me in the direction you need me to go. We'll table this for later." And by *later* she meant *never*. She really didn't want to delve any deeper into Nora's apparent disillusionment. There was enough grief in this house to fill a well. No sense in overflowing the damn thing.

Natalie accepted her offer and pointed down the hallway. "I need someone to help with the guests. More have arrived and I'm stuck in the kitchen. And—" she paused, rubbing her arms together with a brief glance around the room "—make sure you close this door behind you. There's a terrible draft coming in from somewhere."

"Sure," she said. The last thing she wanted to do was usher in more people who no doubt wanted to ask about her long absence, but Natalie was in drill-sergeant mode and trying to back out would only cause her to draw the big guns. Besides, Natalie had pretty much single-handedly put together all the arrangements for the day and the least she could do was point people toward the food and accept a few condolences.

Drawing a deep breath, she followed Natalie and re-entered the family room, where people she recognized and some she didn't milled around or huddled in clusters. Skirting the larger groups, she fielded a few questions, but for the most part, she was left alone. The guests were respectfully brief in their innocent questioning, and Tasha was soon relaxed enough to consider grabbing a bite from the buffet table. Plate in hand, she noted with a start she was standing right beside Josh. Seeing him at the cemetery had been shocking enough, but being in such close proximity that she could smell the crisp scent of his aftershave and see the subtle touch of time in his face caused an irrational longing to lay her head on his shoulder. She knew it was Natalie who invited him, but she hadn't expected him to accept.

Moving quietly, she tried leaving the buffet table, but Josh caught her movement out of the corner of his eye and turned.

They stared, each wondering what to say to each other, until Tasha realized what they were doing was childish. They were adults; time to act like it. She braved a small smile.

"You look good," she admitted in a grudging tone.

He inclined his head, accepting her compliment, and murmured, "I could say the same to you. It seems the jungle agrees with you."

"Thanks," she returned, waiting as he put slices of roast beef and potatoes on his plate and added a slice of buttered bread, then moved away. After loading her own plate, she hesitated and he turned, as if reading her indecision or feeling her reluctance to take a seat beside him. Once they'd been more than friends; now they weren't even acquaintances. He jerked his head in invitation but she knew it was out of courtesy. "Are you sure?"

"It's fine," he assured her, this time with more conviction.

He led her into the rarely used sitting room, as if instinctively knowing that she craved some quiet after the emotional events of the day.

They sat at opposite ends of the loveseat her mother had bought at an estate sale and had considered a steal, and she idly wondered when Josh started liking Mrs. Holt's roast, if only to focus on something other than the feel of her heart beating painfully.

He'd always complained it was tougher than an old shoe. He turned and the question must've flashed in her eyes, for he bent toward her and whispered an answer out of the corner of his mouth.

"She knows where I live."

Tasha laughed. She'd seen Mrs. Holt watching the buffet line like a hawk, noting who had bypassed her contribution and who had dutifully taken some.

A foreign feeling created a warm glow inside her and she had to pop a stuffed mushroom into her mouth before she embarrassed herself.

"Besides, I've realized…it's not that bad," he added in a tone that was entirely too high-pitched for honesty or natural for a man of Josh's considerable size.

"That's not what you used to say."

"Things change," he said, sticking a forkful in his mouth with fake relish. "See? Delicious."

Tasha chuckled when his act faltered as he swallowed, and for the barest of seconds, it felt natural to sit beside him enjoying a meal. Until she glanced down and caught the pale white line encircling his ring finger, reminding her sharply that they had taken different roads without each other. The absence of the ring made her wonder. "I heard you married Carrie Porter," she ventured, surprised at how after so many years the knowledge still managed to burn. But she didn't blame him for moving on. Not now, anyway. She popped another mushroom, chewing until a morbid sense of curiosity took hold of her tongue. "Why no ring?"

His mouth formed a grim line and he shrugged. "Didn't figure I should wear the ring anymore when the divorce was final months ago."

Oh. "What happened?"

He shot her a quick look and she got the distinct impression she was trespassing. Heat flooded her cheeks. "Forget it. It's none of my business. I don't know what's gotten into me. Chalk it up to jet lag, grief, pressure from my sisters…take your pick."

He nodded and returned to his plate, leaving her to wonder if she shouldn't just make an exit now before she ended up wandering into dangerous territory for them both.

Time had added lines around his blue eyes, and slivers of gray threaded the hair that had once been solid brown, but his shoulders were wider than she remembered and thick with muscle that hadn't been there when they were kids. As far as she could tell, there was nothing boylike about the man next to her. The knowledge gave her a dark thrill that immediately put her on guard. She wasn't supposed to feel those kinds of things for Josh anymore. But when he was sitting within arm's length, it was hard to ignore the spark.

He surprised her when he started talking about his life with Carrie.

"It was good for a while, but I guess we grew apart. You know how that happens." He paused, but he didn't really expect an answer. "Anyway, she still lives in Stockton. I needed a fresh start and figured I could find that from home. So, here I am."

She nodded, surprised at the modicum of sympathy that she felt for Carrie. "I'm sorry," she offered, hoping Josh knew she was sincere. He accepted her condolences in the same fashion she'd accepted his—politely—and crumpled his soiled napkin before dropping it to his empty plate. As she watched him, a flood of memories came back and Tasha spoke before her brain could catch up and tell her to stop. "You know, when I heard you and Carrie had married…I have to admit, it threw me a little." More than a little, but that fact made little difference now. When he looked at her sharply, she shrugged. "I mean, I guess I never would've put the two of you together because you weren't exactly friends in high school."

"I know." He shrugged again, but the blue of his eyes had gone bleak and she sensed the pain that he was trying to hide. That she could see it so easily jarred her, and she struggled to recover without letting on how it had affected her. It wasn't right that she could still read him so well. Time should've blunted that ability, but it hadn't. He drew himself up, his plate resting in one hand, and briefly met her wide-eyed gaze. "What are you gonna do?" he asked rhetorically, the sarcasm in his tone at odds with what she knew of his personality. "Marriages end every day. I should've known better in the first place."

"What do you mean?" she asked. At one time he'd been quite romantic. Josh was the kind of man women loved to marry because he was a one-woman kind of guy who cherished the family. His bitterness caused sadness to spill over inside her for the boy who'd lost his belief in love.

"Forget it. It's nothing I want to talk about."

"I'm sorry," she said softly, knowing her words were inadequate.

"What's done is done," he said. Their eyes met again, and Tasha was tempted to look away for fear of catching something else that he hadn't meant to share, but she couldn't. Her heart fluttered but she held his gaze, wondering how he managed to affect her after all these years. It was heady and frightening. And it made her question whether or not he shared her ability and could read the confusion she felt. Shaking his head, Josh broke the spell, and when he spoke again, at least the sarcasm was gone. "Everything happens for a reason, right?"

"That's what some people believe."

"You don't?" he said, catching what she didn't say.

"No." She left it at that and he didn't press.

"Well, I'm one of those people, because if hooking up with Carrie was good for only one thing, I got it, and that's my son."

Son? An overwhelming sense of self-pity filled her. "You have a son?" she asked, forcing her voice to stay light and politely interested when she felt cheated of something that never truly belonged to her in the first place. "What's his name?"

"Christopher," he answered. "He's fourteen."

"Just one?" she asked, remembering a distant conversation held between two young lovers seeking shelter from a summer storm in an abandoned hay barn. Back then, he'd boasted of wanting a houseful of Halvorsen sons and daughters.

"Just one," he confirmed, though there was regret in his voice. "Carrie had problems with her pregnancy and we didn't want to risk it."

"That was smart," Tasha said.

"Yeah, well, it helped that Carrie wasn't interested in more kids, anyway. She said one was enough, and since it was so hard for her, I agreed." He turned to her, a speculative light in his eyes as he abruptly switched subjects. "So, what have you been up to all this time? I heard something about the Peace

Corps? That's intense. I always knew you'd do great things. Seems I wasn't wrong."

The proud statement, touched with wistfulness, made her stomach flop in an uncomfortable manner. She didn't deserve his praise, or anyone else's for that matter. She enjoyed her work—it gave her a measure of peace knowing she was helping others to lead a better life—but her motivation hadn't been grounded in humanitarian reasons. It had simply been the fastest and easiest way to escape the nightmares, the guilt and the questions. The fact that it had turned out to be something she could embrace without reservation was just a perk.

"Anyone can join the Peace Corps. It's not an exclusive club or anything. You just have to want to help people," she said, suddenly hating that her life had been shattered before she'd had the chance to actually live it. Surprised by the odd burst of rancor, she covered with a light laugh, adding with false brevity, "Oh, and not have a phobia for really big bugs. And snakes. The jungle is full of them. Most are harmless, the bugs that is, and even edible. Many indigenous tribes find grubs delicious. I've even tried a few," she admitted with a blush. "Some taste like popcorn when roasted over an open fire."

"Popcorn?"

"Well, sort of. I don't think they're going to replace Orville Redenbacher anytime soon, but they're…crunchy and full of protein."

He stared at her for a moment before breaking into a loud guffaw that took her by surprise. At first she felt defensive, but once she realized he wasn't laughing at her but rather at the very odd conversation turn, she joined him. Wiping at her eyes, she said, "I'm sorry…that was a really weird thing to say at a wake…."

"Hey, no need to apologize. I totally understand." The warmth of his voice told her somehow he did understand and she relaxed for the first time since touching down in California. She missed this feeling and it was tempting to sink into it, but she knew it was created out of extreme circumstances. What they'd had was gone. She wasn't foolish enough to hope that they could ever recreate what they'd both destroyed.

The splash of reality drowned the good feelings she'd been enjoying and brought her back to earth.

He'd married Carrie, and Tasha had run away, afraid of what people would say, think or feel when they found out what had happened to Emmett's

Mill's sweetheart. An even worse thought would've been if they didn't believe her.

Her own father hadn't. Why would anyone else?

It'd been easier to run. And, as she sat beside Josh, she realized she'd never truly stopped running.

He didn't know what happened that night; he'd already left Emmett's Mill with Carrie to start a new life without her.

Even so, she'd cried his name into her pillow, wishing for his strong arms to calm her quaking body and chase away the nightmares that came every night, no matter how hard she pushed herself, hoping for oblivion.

But that was long ago and she was a different person now.

And she would die before she ever divulged to anyone, much less Josh, what had happened to her.

CHAPTER THREE

TASHA HELPED CLEAR DISHES with her sisters, her mind a jumbled mess, happy to avoid conversation with her father, though a surreptitious glance in his direction where he sat stone-faced and bereft should've told her he was in no shape to resurrect old arguments. For that matter, neither was she.

"I think that went fairly well," Natalie said, loading the dishwasher while Tasha hand washed what wouldn't fit.

"As well as a wake can go, I suppose," she murmured, pausing to rub wearily at her left eye with her wrist and sneaking another glance at her father.

"Where did such a weird custom start, anyway? Bringing food to a bunch of grieving people. Stupid, if you ask me," Nora said, mostly to Natalie, who to her credit only reacted with a long-suffering look. "I, for one, didn't feel like chowing down after my mother's funeral. Morbid. Simply morbid."

The last words were delivered as she stalked from

the room to gather the rest of the leftovers, and Tasha was glad for the respite. She hadn't remembered Nora being such a hothead.

"You sure you don't mind hand washing?" Natalie asked, drawing her attention.

"I can do this in my sleep. No dishwashers where I'm stationed," she answered with a sigh, placing the cleaned pot on the dish rack and proceeding to the next. "Besides, it feels good to do something. Makes me feel useful."

"You were a big help today," Natalie said, brooking an amused smile on her part. Nat was always trying to make everyone feel better. Tasha accepted the compliment and finished with the dishes. Silence stretched between them and Tasha tumbled into an odd funk that probably had more to do with her jet lag than her grief, as the true measure of that emotion hadn't quite hit her yet.

Her two younger sisters had grown into strong, capable women while she was away. Not that she'd doubted they would, but Nora was still in high school and Natalie was in her sophomore year at UC Davis when she left, and Tasha hadn't been thinking about the future, theirs or her own. She'd run away with little thought to anything but escape, and while she'd been running, time had kept moving. She stole a glance at her sister and withheld the bitter sigh trapped in her chest with the rest of the terrible and awful things she kept hidden away.

A tear slid down her nose before she could stop it, and a wave of sorrow threatened to knock the strength out of her legs. Bracing herself against the sink, she prayed for the ability to get through this moment before Natalie noticed the breakdown that was surely heading her way. *Breathe. Just breathe.* But a sob caught in her throat and an ugly sound escaped.

"Tasha?"

Turning away, she closed her eyes, but the action only squeezed out the tears she was trying to hold back. "I need some air," she managed to say before bolting from the room. Flying past Nora, who was just returning with more empty plates, she stepped into the darkness and embraced the frosty air as it penetrated her clothing and caressed her skin.

Sinking to the front porch step, she wrapped her arms around herself, more for reassurance than warmth, and fought to stay focused. Her breath came in painful stops and starts as she willed the hurt away. She was too old to keep saying *it's not fair,* but that didn't keep her from thinking it over and over. Wiping at the tears that felt frozen to her cheek, she stared up at the sky and wondered if her mother was up there somewhere. And if so, was she looking down at her eldest daughter with a sad frown on her face? Wondering how her brightest star had winked out within a heartbeat?

She dropped her head to rest on her knees and tried curling into a ball. *I'm sorry I didn't come home earlier. I would've been here for you.* Fresh tears slid down her cheek and her gaze was lost on the darkened landscape of her parents' home. She drew a shaky breath and buried her face into her arms.

Oh, Mama…I'm so sorry.

JOSH GRABBED A POT HOLDER and pulled the smoking mess out of the oven just as Christopher's lanky form rounded the kitchen corner to lounge against the wall. Damn.

"Another one bites the dust?"

Pot holder covering his mouth as he coughed and sputtered, he gave his son a short nod. "Looks like pizza again. Sorry, buddy."

"Fine by me." Christopher sent a dubious look toward what had started out as Tater Tots casserole but had ended charred and dangerous, and said, "Did that even start out worth eating?"

Josh wrinkled his nose at the concoction and pursed his lips. "Dunno." He swung around to give his son a grin. "But I get points for trying, right?"

"Sure, Dad," Christopher said, cracking the first grin Josh had seen on his son's face since they moved. Christopher pivoted on his heel and Josh followed him out of the kitchen, glad to leave behind the burning wreckage and needing to see how Christopher was adjusting.

"So, you getting used to the new school yet?" he asked, rubbing at the sting in his eyes and blinking hard until his vision cleared. "Everything okay? No one's giving you any trouble?"

"It's *fine*," Christopher answered, his cheeks reddening when his adolescent voice cracked.

"You'd tell me if it wasn't, right?"

"Dad, stop stressing. I'm fine. One school's no different than the other. They all suck."

His hopes sank at Christopher's revealing comment. He'd hoped Emmett's Mill would be a fresh start for the both of them. At the last school, Christopher had been bullied incessantly. It wasn't the same as when Josh was in school. These kids weren't just stealing lunch money or tossing nerds in trash cans. With the last incident, a group of punks had cornered Christopher, flashing a switchblade.

Josh felt sick all over again at the thought of what might've happened if a teacher hadn't come upon them. Suspensions had been given to the boys from the school's side, and after Josh filed a complaint with the police, felony charges had been levied. By that point, he'd already packed his bags, finished with everything associated with the city of Stockton. Including his wife.

Speaking of. He withheld the grimace and tried to keep his voice neutral. "It's your mom's weekend. She'll be here Friday after school. Make sure you have your stuff ready."

"What's the point? She won't come."

Josh winced inwardly at the hurt couched inside his son's belligerence. Since moving, Carrie hadn't made much of an effort to see Christopher. He knew the reason, but he'd hoped Christopher didn't. "She'll come," Josh said. "She promised."

"She promised last weekend, too," Christopher reminded him, his young face darkening. "She's too busy spending her new boyfriend's money."

Josh should've known Christopher would catch on to the real reason Carrie found one excuse after another to reschedule her visitation. He was a smart kid. But as Josh struggled for some sort of reason to give his son this time, he needn't have bothered. Christopher wasn't interested in listening.

"Who cares? I don't," Christopher said, slouching against the wall as if he really didn't care if his mother came to see him or not. "She can't stand me, anyway."

"That's not true," Josh said. "She loves you."

"Actions speak louder than words, Dad," Christopher said with a healthy dose of sarcasm before shoving off the wall and walking away, obviously finished with the conversation.

Josh's heart cracked just a little bit more for what his son was going through. The fact of the matter was, Carrie made it no secret that Christopher embarrassed her. She'd expected their son would be athletic and popular because his father had been, but instead, he was gawky and awkward, his body leaning toward scrawny. To make things worse, early-childhood asthma had made him unable to do many of the things other kids were doing at his age, and he wore braces and glasses. Add to the mix a healthy dose of natural shyness and he made a perfect target for bullies.

Josh knew Carrie loved their son, but she was too wrapped up in things that didn't matter to realize she was losing her only child. But Josh was the last person Carrie would accept parental advice from. The divorce was too fresh; the hurt and disillusionment too overwhelming—he wouldn't even try. Either she'd wise up, or not. All he could do was to be there for Christopher.

Awash with regret for choices he had made when he was young, he knew in his heart that somehow fate had made him and Tasha take separate paths for a reason. But right now, he couldn't help wondering how things might've been different if they'd been able to make a long-distance relationship work.

Stanford hadn't seemed that far away. He'd been so proud of Tasha for getting into the prestigious school. Although the distance eventually tore them apart, he never stopped being proud of his smart girl—even if she wasn't his anymore.

Ah, hell. He scrubbed his hands across his face in annoyance at the wistful direction of his thoughts. There was no use in looking backward all the time, and he made a point to avoid it even though Carrie always accused him of holding a torch for Tasha. It wasn't true and no amount of reassuring ever seemed to convince her. He'd given everything to his marriage. But his best wasn't enough. A failed marriage was a helluva wake-up call.

He'd come home to Emmett's Mill to get his head on straight, and that's exactly what he was going to do. When his older brother, Dean, had offered him a job at Halvorsen Construction, he'd gladly accepted, more than happy to bury himself in hard labor, to earn every bruise, scab and aching muscle.

He hadn't factored in Tasha. Didn't think he had to. From what he gathered, she rarely came home.

Until now.

He grimaced at the weakness he felt slowly building when he thought of her. She still had the power to make his insides do weird, girlie things, and that was enough to make him realize it was best to steer clear.

That shouldn't be too hard, he thought, noting his sharp disappointment. He sighed softly. It didn't look as if Tasha was itching to return for good.

CHAPTER FOUR

TASHA GAVE THE LIST in her hand a quick glance as she breezed through the double sliding doors of the small grocery market, intent on finishing the task as quickly as she could. She wasn't thrilled with doing the grocery shopping, but both her sisters had plans of their own and couldn't change them.

Miner Market hadn't changed much since she was a kid, she noted, going right to the deli counter for her father's roast beef. In high school, she used to come here with her girlfriends for a hot burrito and a soda, which was often shared among them during lunch. She smiled at the memory and kept moving until she heard her named called.

"Tasha Simmons! Look at you! Goodness, girl, don't you age?"

Tasha stopped and a name filtered into her memory as the brunette woman ran over to her. "Crystal, wow. You look great, too. How are you?" she inquired politely.

She patted a rounded stomach and beamed. "Can't complain. Number three right here. Another boy. Jack said pretty soon we'll have our own basketball team at the rate we're going. Any kids for you?"

"Uh, no," she answered, struggling to keep her expression pleasantly bland, ignoring the void she felt in her heart. "Not yet." Probably never. She lifted her basket. "Well, good to see you. I'd better get to this list or Natalie will kill me."

Crystal nodded and moved her cart as if to leave but stopped as a sudden thought occurred to her. "I heard Josh's in town, too. Have you seen him?"

"Actually, yes, he came to my mother's funeral."

Crystal's expression lost some of its sparkle. "Oh, that's right. She was such an awesome woman," she said, resting her hand on her belly. "You let me know if you guys need anything. Anything at all."

Tasha accepted Crystal's offer with a nod but knew she wouldn't call.

She detoured down the bread aisle when she saw someone else she'd gone to school with and exhaled softly in relief when she didn't hear her name called at her back.

For a fleeting, selfish moment, she wished she was already back in Belize, away from the groups of well-meaning folk who had no idea why she wasn't in the mood to reminisce.

Her coworkers knew she treasured her private time, and since she'd never established herself as the social type, they left her to it.

She drew a deep breath against the sudden tightness in her chest and looked down at the few items she'd managed to grab and groaned. The list was a page long. How much food could one old man eat? She had a sneaking suspicion Natalie had loaded the list in the hopes that she'd run into a friend or two. She sighed. Her sister wasn't as sly as she thought. Tasha's problem wasn't Emmett's Mill or the people; it was the memory. She'd seen countless counselors, psychiatrists and even a shaman or two in the hopes of dealing with that one incident, but her own brand of therapy prescribed avoidance. And it worked. She didn't see the point of messing with a method that wasn't broken.

Almost finished and grumbling under her breath about retribution, she rounded the corner and almost swallowed her tongue when she came face-to-face with someone she'd hoped to never see again.

Diane Lewis, Bronson's wife, stood not more than four feet in front of her, an uncomfortable expression on her pinched face. For a paralyzing moment, Tasha thought Diane knew what had happened, but when she calmed, she realized Bronson would never have admitted his guilt. Still, Diane's reaction to her wasn't kind, which made her wonder what story Bronson had given for her sudden departure.

"Hello, Diane," she ventured, offering a smile.

"Natasha." Diane returned with her given name instead of the shortened version everyone else used. "You look well."

"Thank you." She struggled to find neutral ground but her insides were trembling. A condolence was in order for Bronson's death but she couldn't find the words. When Natalie wrote to tell her, Tasha had read the letter multiple times and crumpled it to her chest as she allowed grim satisfaction to roll through her. It wasn't right, certainly wasn't Christian-like, but she hoped he rotted in hell. And it wasn't something she could tell his wife. Diane solved the dilemma by speaking again first.

"I heard about your mother. Give Gerald my best."

Tasha nodded, and Diane, stiff-backed and elegantly coiffed, kept moving. It was several moments before Tasha could breathe without great effort. Wiping at her eyes, she glanced quickly to see if anyone had caught the uncomfortable exchange. Once satisfied she'd suffered alone, she hastened for the checkout lane.

TASHA RETURNED TO HER dad's place and heard her sisters' voices, one raised and one exasperated.

"What's going on?" she asked, and placed the groceries on the kitchen counter. Nora immediately crossed her arms and sent a stony look her way, while Natalie simply exhaled, the breath lifting her bangs as frustration laced her features. "What now?" She followed her sister's gaze outside. Their father was on the porch swing without benefit of a jacket or sweater and the wind was kicking up. "What's he doing? It's freezing. Someone needs to get him to come inside."

"What a novel idea. Why didn't we think of that?" Nora quipped sarcastically, continuing with a snort. "Like we haven't already tried. He won't budge. It's like he's gone crazy or something."

"Cut him some slack. He just lost his wife," Tasha reminded her sister sharply, and moved past them. What was Nora's problem? Everyone in the family was hurting. Was it asking too much for her to be a little more sensitive? Bracing herself against the cold, she stalked out the side door to the porch swing, still annoyed at Nora for her callousness but not quite sure what to say to her father. They'd pretty much avoided each other since she returned, and while it hurt to be treated like the plague, she didn't have the courage to push it.

As she came closer she saw his eyes were blood-shot and softly swollen from tears, and her heart stuttered. She slowed her step and gingerly sat beside him.

"Dad?" She tried to discern what he was looking at, but she saw nothing except pine trees and bracken. She turned to him. "What's going on? You need to come inside. It's too cold."

His bottom lip, blue from the frigid mountain air, trembled as if he were about to answer, but nothing came out. Instead, he lifted his chin just a bit higher as he focused on a point just beyond the pines.

She tried again, ignoring the goose bumps rioting across any exposed skin and the rush of memories that threatened to rob her of her ability to speak coherently. Once, this man had been her hero. Until the day he failed her when she needed him the most. *Not the time.* Focus on the now before the man froze to death. "Dad, please come inside. Natalie's made your favorite for dinner. Meat loaf, I think."

"Not hungry," he retorted hoarsely.

Stubborn man. "What are you doing? Trying to die of exposure? Don't be like this. Mom's gone. We don't need to lose our father in the same week because he was too foolish to come in before a storm."

"Don't talk to me about losing your mom," he said, startling her with his sharp, angry rasp. His mouth tightened and his hand trembled as he lifted it to wipe away a sudden glint in his eye. "You weren't here when she needed you. You don't know what she went through."

Stricken by the vehemence in her father's voice, she tripped on her own words as she tried to defend herself. "Dad, I—"

"Bah!" he spat. "Go save a goddamned tree. It's all you seem to care about."

"That's not true and you know it," she gasped. "Why would you say that? I came home as soon as I found out."

"She was already dead!"

Tasha sucked in a sharp breath and tears sprang to her eyes. Once again her own father was against her. How could he possibly believe she wouldn't have been here if she'd known sooner? "I came as soon as I could," she said, trying her best to keep her voice level when she wanted to scream.

"She cried your name over and over, wanting to know why you weren't here." He buried his head in his hands, raking his fingers through the wild knot of white hair on his head, his breath catching as he continued. "And there was nothing I could do. Nothing! Natalie called and left messages with your supervisor. She wrote letters… Why would you hurt your mother like that? She needed you so much," he ended with a bereaved moan, his shoulders shaking silently as he cried into his hands.

She'd never received any messages. A million different things could've happened to them, none of which were anyone's fault specifically, but the communication gaps were wider in underdeveloped countries. She squeezed her eyes shut and hated her sisters for sending her outside to be crucified. But she couldn't argue the facts. Tasha hadn't been here when her family needed her the most. She risked rejection and gently placed her hand on her father's shoulder. "I'm sorry it wasn't good enough. Sorrier than anyone will ever know," she added in a whisper. "I can't take it back. I'd do anything if I could. Deep down somewhere, you have to believe that, Dad. I loved her, too."

His throat worked convulsively as he raised his head, searching for the truth in her eyes. *Please believe…*

After a long moment he nodded and tears of relief sprang to her eyes, but she choked them back for her father's sake. He was drowning in a sea of his own heartache, and she wouldn't do anything to further drag him under, but she yearned to hear something else from him—something she was not likely to get.

"Oh, Tasha… My Missy…she died in so much pain." He looked away, but not before she caught the open anguish in his heart. Fresh guilt washed over her. She tried to speak, to offer something to ease the burden he carried, but nothing short of a watery croak came out. Say something, her brain urged, but she didn't know what to say. She knew nothing would ease his sense of loss, because she knew nothing anyone could say to her would mend the jagged hole in her heart. *So it was better to just sit there and freeze your ass off?* "Dad, please come in out of the cold. Everyone is worried you're going to catch pneumonia out here. Please."

A long moment passed before her words reached

that closed-off space blocked by his grief, then he turned slowly, a measure of his old personality asserting itself in his gruff voice. "You go on. I'll come in when I'm ready," he said, dismissing her.

She blew a hard breath in mild frustration. "Dad, Nat and Nora sent me out here to bring you in. If I go back in there without you, either they'll just send me out again or Nat will send Nora, and trust me when I say that girl is not big on saying things nice. She's likely to have you declared mentally unfit and put in one of those old-folk homes where they feed you nothing but Jell-O and Ritz crackers. You don't want that, do you?"

A part of her was joking, but another part had to admit that sometimes Nora was unpredictable. She wouldn't put it past her sister to do something so rash, if only to make a point.

Her father's chuckle sounded dry and rusty but she welcomed the sound. He rose on stiff limbs from the old porch. "That girl has balls the size of Texas sometimes," he said.

"She reminds me of someone else I know," she retorted under her breath, fatigue suddenly pulling at her eyes and forcing a yawn despite the chatter of her teeth. She followed her father into the house, glad to be out of the cold and to have accomplished her objective.

The minute they came inside, Natalie fussed around their father, trying to put a shawl across his shoulders until he waved her away and announced he was going to bed, leaving Nora to stare after him in hard-edged annoyance and Natalie to groan over all the food she'd just prepared.

"Tasha, can't you talk to him? He needs to eat," Natalie implored, ignoring Nora's muttered comments even as she looked in the direction their father had disappeared. "I'm worried about him. He hasn't eaten a good meal in days."

She sighed wearily and grabbed her coat. "Nat, I think he needs a little space. He's dealing with a lot right now. It's not every day your life is destroyed, you know. You can't expect a raging appetite when everything you've ever known is gone."

"I understand how he feels…" Somehow, Tasha doubted that, but there was no point in arguing and even if there was, she didn't have the energy. Natalie ignored Tasha's sigh and continued, "But even so, he needs to eat."

"He'll eat when he's hungry. Just wrap everything up and leave it in the fridge," she suggested, sliding her arm into her coat, eager to seek the solitude of her hotel room.

Nora came into the room and eyed Tasha's state of dress with a gathering frown. "Where are you going?"

"Back to my hotel," she answered.

"I don't think so. We have details to discuss."

Natalie stepped forward but Nora ignored her, her voice rising as she crossed her arms across her chest. "You're not running out on us again when we need you the most."

"I'm not running out on you," she returned brusquely, rubbing at her eyes with the flat of her palm. "I'm tired and I want to go to bed."

"We're all tired, Tasha. But we need to talk about a few things."

"Like what?"

"Like who's going to go through Mom's things, who's going to help Dad with the day-to-day stuff, you know, things like that." Foreboding tingled at the edge of her thoughts as she waited for her sister to get to the point. "And—" she lifted her chin, as if knowing what she was about to say was going to go over like something icky in a punch bowl "—we need to decide how to split up the shifts."

"Shifts? What are you talking about?"

Natalie jumped in even as she shot Nora a look that said she wasn't happy with her delivery, clarifying, "Tasha, what Nora is trying to tell you is we need you home for a while—"

"I can't," she broke in flatly. "I have to return to Belize in a few days. I have projects, people who depend on me. My team is right in the middle of creating a serviceable water-treatment system and I can't just drop everything because—"

"Because our mother died?" Nora finished for her, two high points of angry color flashing in her cheeks. "No, heaven forbid, that Tasha rearrange her schedule to accommodate a death in the family." She threw up her hands and stalked into the kitchen, still ranting. "Gotta make sure some obscure village in the jungle has running water or else Tasha might lose her saintly status."

"What's her problem?" Tasha queried Natalie, who was looking as if she were caught between the proverbial rock and a hard place. "She's been pissed off at me since I returned. I don't understand what she's so angry about."

Natalie took a seat on the armrest of the sofa, something she never would've done if their mother was still around, and sighed. "This is how she deals with her grief, I guess. She turns it into anger."

"Yeah. Anger against me." Tasha exhaled loudly,

then turned to her sister. "But you understand, right? Why I can't stay? I mean, I really do have obligations." Tasha expected a quick answer, but Natalie's long pause made her look sharply. "What? Are you mad at me, too?"

"A little," she admitted, but she seemed ashamed of her admission and elucidated in a quiet voice. "I know why you wouldn't return before…but the man who hurt you died five years ago, Tasha, and Mom needed you." Her voice cracked a little and tears glistened as she added, "We all needed you. And now that you're back, we need you to stay at least long enough to get Dad back on track."

Stay? Here? "I could lose my post," she blurted out, hoping to appeal to Natalie's more pragmatic side. When Natalie's expression didn't soften, Tasha knew she wasn't going to back down. "What if I can't?" she asked, knowing Natalie would understand she was talking about more than just helping out around the house. "What if it's just too much? Being here makes it real all over again." She lowered her voice to a painful whisper. "I ran into Diane Lewis at the store."

Natalie's face softened. "What did she say?"

"Not a lot," she admitted. "But it was incredibly

awkward and…I don't want to go through those kinds of encounters on a daily basis."

"I understand." Natalie came toward her and pulled her into a fierce hug. "But you're not alone. We'll be with you every step, every moment. And if anyone, including Diane Lewis, even looks cross-eyed at you, we'll handle it. You can't keep running. We need this. *You* need this," she stressed softly, sending a sharp pang straight to Tasha's heart. "There's more to your past than just that one ugly moment. We're in there, too."

Tasha wanted to say no, but words failed her and she nodded slowly, even though her instincts told her to board the first plane to Belize, back to the place where no one knew her secrets or wanted to know more than she was willing to share. Where no one expected her to face a past that she'd willfully buried under layers of denial, anger and grief.

Her sisters were asking more than she could give.

Yet, she felt her head nod. "Fine," she whispered, turning to leave but adding a caveat for sanity's sake. "Only until things are settled. No exceptions."

"It must be nice to be able to drop limitations on your family. Makes me wonder if you do the same thing to your people in the Peace Corps," Nora said, returning to the room, her eyes hot. "I'll bet you trip all over yourself to help out when it doesn't involve us."

Tasha drew back in stricken silence, unable to breathe from the pain in her heart from Nora's attack. But it was true. Tasha ran herself ragged when she was working, trying to dull the constant hurt she carried with her from day to day. Her mouth worked but nothing came out, words failed her. If only she had the courage to explain. Tasha was spared the effort for Natalie whirled on Nora, surprising them both.

"Stop it! I've had enough of your snap judgments on a person you hardly know."

"Why are you taking her side?" Nora wailed. "Ever since she got here she's been trying to skip out on us like we've got the goddamned plague! Why are you defending her?"

Tasha started to say something, but Natalie stopped her with a gentle hand on her arm. Natalie drew a deep breath, and when she began again, her tone softened. "She's agreed to stay long enough to help us get things settled with Dad. Just stop treating her like she's the enemy. She's our sister. Try to remember that fact."

The glitter in Nora's eyes betrayed the hurt she was feeling, but her expression hardened just the same. "Yeah, well somebody ought to remind her of that fact, too," she spat, then turned and grabbed her own jacket. "Food's put away. I'm outta here."

"Nora…" Tasha managed to croak her sister's name but the rest died on her lips. Their father's snores filtered down the hallway and she was glad he hadn't witnessed their meltdown. She met Natalie's weary look. "I don't want to come between you two. You guys are close and I don't want to ruin it. She has a right to be angry."

"I agree," Natalie said quietly. "But she takes it to another level. That's her way with most things, but it shouldn't be the way she is with you. The good news is her temper usually burns out as quickly as it fires. Give it a little time. She'll come around."

"I don't know, Nat." Tasha shook her head wearily. "I don't think there's enough time in the world for Nora to get over her issues with me."

Natalie crooked a thin smile. "Ye of little faith," she said, adding ruefully, "Then again, you might be right."

Tasha's mouth curved for a moment. "Thanks, Nat. Thanks for…everything."

"What are sisters for?" Natalie joked softly before checking her watch. "It's late. I better get going and make sure Evan put Colton to bed."

"He's such a sweet little boy," Tasha murmured,

watching as Natalie shrugged into her coat. "You're lucky to have him."

Natalie smiled, the first bright and genuine one Tasha had seen on her sister's face since arriving in Emmett's Mill. They walked to the door in silence until Natalie, hand on the doorknob, stopped with a sad contemplative look. "You know, I never realized how Mom kept us all connected. She was the common thread. Now I guess it falls to you."

"Oh, God, Nat. Don't set me up to fail. I think I've disappointed enough people to last a lifetime," she said around the lump of fear in her throat.

Natalie ran the back of her hand lovingly against her cheek and graced her with a sweet smile that spoke of her confidence in Tasha and said, "You won't fail. It's not in your nature. You're a leader… always have been and always will be."

Tasha stared, struggling under the weight of her sister's belief and her own denial, but most of all, she wasn't sure if she wanted her sister to be right or wrong.

CHAPTER FIVE

JOSH MADE HIS WAY toward the local newspaper office to start a subscription. He enjoyed reading the newspaper on Sunday morning with his coffee. It gave him a sense of normalcy that he felt sadly lacking since his divorce, and, small as it was, he was clinging to it.

The storm had broken, and although a bracing wind kept pedestrians clutching at their jackets to ward off the chill, Josh barely felt the cold. His mind was crowded with the details of reestablishing himself. Dean was good enough to offer him a job on his crew, and Josh was happy to work with his brothers again.

They were good guys, and Dean had a son a little older than Christopher who was willing to help his younger cousin get acclimated to the new school.

Gripping the handle, the cold burning into his palm, he pushed the door open and walked inside.

The blond receptionist looked up at the sound of the door jingling, and when she saw who it was, a bright yet surprised smile lit her face. "Josh Halvorsen? Wow! It's been forever since I last saw *you*."

"Patti Jenkins," he said slowly with recognition, following with a warm smile. Patti had been one of those girls he knew peripherally, but as they hadn't exactly traveled in the same circles in school, he hadn't gone out of his way to really know her. But he did remember her being a nice girl. Real smart, too. "Since when'd you start working for the *Tribune*?" he asked, happy enough to make small talk as he handed her the cutout from an old newspaper for new subscriptions.

"Oh, about three years ago. I was working for the bank, but then there were some layoffs so I ended up here. It's nice enough and I get benefits. That's all that matters." She glanced at the paperwork. "You moving home for good?"

"Seems that way. The city really wasn't my scene. Too much country in this ol' boy."

She gave him an appraising glance, answering cheekily, "Nothing wrong with that. Country's fine by me. I'm one husband away from being single and I'm always looking for the next lucky Mr. Patti Jenkins."

He chuckled, knowing she was kidding, and was happy to play along. "Good to know."

Grinning, she returned to the paperwork in her hand. "It will just take a minute to get you set up, but your first issue will take about two weeks." She waved the paperwork in annoyance. "Something about the file system. I don't know, for some reason, even though we don't have more than a handful of subscriptions it takes longer than molasses in winter to get it going. Though," she added with a wink, "once you're in the system, it'll take an act of God to get you out. I don't think Adeline Merriweather has paid for a subscription in nigh five years, but she gets her weekly paper as faithful as ever." Josh laughed outright at that and she continued with a twinkle in her eye. "Well, honestly, who can take away some sweet old biddy's weekly news? It's just not seemly. Anyway…here you go."

She handed him the receipt and he tucked it into his wallet. He was in midthanks when the door jingled and he turned.

Tasha's expression surely mirrored his own as she shut the door behind her and offered a tentative smile to both Patti and himself. "It seems you're every-where in this small town," she murmured. She peeked around him to wave at Patti. "Hi, Patti. You look great. How've you been?"

"Can't complain. You?"

"Same."

"Don't let her fool you, she's been working for the Peace Corps for the past couple of years," he interjected before his good sense got a hold of his mouth. She blushed at the hint of pride in his voice, and he remembered how shy she could become under the right circumstances.

"I heard you were back in town, too," Patti said, gesturing for him to move out of the way. He pretended to act offended but they knew it was for show. "How are you doing? I'm sorry to hear about your mom."

"Thank you, Patti. It's been a tough transition, especially for Dad."

"I'll bet. If my mom died my dad would probably try to climb into the grave with her," Patti said in commiseration. "He wouldn't know how to function without her. I don't even think he knows how to write a check." A sudden thought occurred to her. "Oh, goodness. I hope to God my parents go at the same time. I don't want to have to teach my dad to balance a checkbook!"

Tasha smiled, though Josh could tell it was plainly for Patti's benefit. She cloaked her sadness well enough, but he knew her better than most. As if remembering herself, Patti asked, "So, what can I do for you today?"

Tasha cleared her throat. "Well, I was wondering if I could get extra copies of my mom's obituary," she asked, then apologized. "I know it seems morbid, but there are some members of our extended family who would like to see it and they won't settle for a photocopy."

Patti waved away her concern. "No problem. How many do you need?" Tasha indicated five and Patti disappeared into the back to retrieve them.

She turned to Josh and he tried not to stare like a starving man, but that's how he was starting to feel.

"So…are you getting settled in?" she asked.

"So far so good. We rented a small place out on Darrah. It's not the Ritz but it's nice enough for me and Chris."

"How's your son adjusting?"

How'd she know to ask the one question he'd like to avoid. "Not as well as I'd hoped," he admitted, surprising himself by answering. But it felt good to talk to Tasha. He couldn't deny it. "He's a shy kid, likes his computers more than anything else. It's hard for him to make friends sometimes."

"Natalie was like that," she murmured.

He nodded, remembering. "I'd forgotten how awkward she was." He chuckled. "She was an odd bird for a while."

"Tell me about it." Tasha's light laughter followed. "I thought she'd never come out of that phase. She practically lived with her nose in a book, though in hindsight, she now owns a beautiful children's bookstore so I suppose it was all for a reason."

"I guess I shouldn't worry about my son and his love for computers, then, huh?"

"He could be the next Bill Gates," she offered. "You never know."

"No, you're right. I'll stop worrying."

Patti reentered the room talking. "Must've been a popular newsweek. You got our last saleable copies," Patti said with a surprised shake of her head then a shrug. "Never can tell what's going to get these people's motor running. The weeks you think you're going to sell out, you have extra. The week you think is going to be slow…sells out. Go figure."

"Thanks, Patti," she said, handing over a crisp five dollar bill.

"No problem."

Tasha pulled the copies close to her chest, and after a long pause, the corner of her mouth lifted in goodbye and she left.

"It's amazing. She almost looks the same as when we were in school," Patti observed, then turned a speculative look his way. "You know, everyone thought you guys were going to end up together. The high-school sweetheart thing. Shocked the whole town when you married Carrie Porter. But, then, I guess it's true what they say. You can't help who you fall in love with."

He didn't have a reply that wasn't tainted with the bitterness he often felt, so he smiled and thanked her for the help and the conversation.

Striding to his truck, he resisted the urge to look in the direction Tasha left, irritated with his desire to do so.

He slid into the driver's seat and started the truck. As he pulled onto the main street, he put Tasha out of his head and focused on the day ahead. Dean had a job lined up for him and he was glad for the distraction. He didn't need Tasha in his head or his heart.

TASHA DROVE WITH EVERY intention of returning to her parents' place, but seeing Josh yet again had made her restless. Time had treated him kindly, unlike some of their other classmates. No male-pattern balding being hidden under a ball cap, such as the case with Tommy Reynolds, whom she'd run into yesterday while at the post office. No, Josh had gone from impishly cute to maturely handsome, and she'd have to be blind not to notice. She tried not to care. But there was something about Josh that still managed to take her breath away even when she was trying her best to stay detached.

Sometimes, late at night, when the angry buzz of mosquitoes just outside the net draped over her bed kept sleep at bay, her thoughts drifted to him and the memory of her first and, judging by her transient relationships since, only love.

It seemed cosmically cruel that they were in Emmett's Mill at the same time. Seeing him again only reminded her of what might have been. And she hated it.

Unlike her peers, who'd boasted at graduation that they couldn't wait to get out of their tiny town, Tasha had known once she graduated from Stanford she'd come back. It was all planned out in her mind. Of course, at seventeen she'd been a bit naive. There wasn't much call for an anthropologist in Emmett's

Mill unless she wanted to parlay her expensive education into a teaching position at the high school. And, she'd figured that she and Josh would make their home—complete with a white picket fence and marigolds planted along the cobblestone walkway—somewhere here, but she hadn't figured out what Josh would do for a living, either. Josh hadn't shown any interest in going to college, but she'd always assumed that she could talk him into going to community college, at least while she was at Stanford.

A small, disgusted sound escaped her as she drove, wondering how she'd ever been so innocent. Nothing had turned out the way she'd planned in her head.

Before she realized where she was going, she turned down Crystal Aire Drive and cruised past the law offices of Parker and Dalton, formerly known as Lewis, Parker and Dalton before Bronson Lewis died five years ago.

She swallowed the painful lump in her throat and willed her heartbeat to slow to a normal rate. He couldn't hurt her. He was dead. But seeing the scene of the crime again made a fine sheen of sweat bead her upper lip despite the winter chill in the air, and her fingers curled around the steering wheel tight enough to make the leather squeal in protest. She avoided this place for a reason. She had no problem seeing herself at twenty-two, walking past the receptionists with a grin, chatting animatedly about her adventures in college life, flashing bright smiles at someone she'd always considered a family friend.

Her father's best friend.

A shudder traveled through her body painfully and she pushed her foot down on the gas pedal, anxious to get away from the memory and the humiliation that was always there under the surface for being so dumb, so trusting and so easily a victim.

CHAPTER SIX

THE NEXT DAY ALL THREE sisters stood staring at the same thing, unable to quite comprehend what they were seeing.

Nora was the first to recover, pointing wildly. "What the *hell* is that?"

Natalie stammered. "I think…it's where the draft is coming from."

"You think?" Nora's dry retort only echoed what Tasha was thinking, but the bewildered expression on Natalie's face had kept her silent. Her poor sister looked on the verge of tears as they all stared at the giant, gaping hole in the side of their parents' house covered with plastic sheeting and secured with duct tape, all wondering the same thing.

"I take it nobody knew about this?" Tasha ventured cautiously, and was rewarded with a shake of Natalie's head. Tasha exhaled slowly. "Okay, that brings me to my next question…how is that no one noticed a hole in the hobby room?"

Natalie stood rigid, her fists clenched tightly at her side as she bit out the words. "Dad always kept this door closed. He's very private so I never even thought about it. And then, with Mom so sick…"

"Why didn't Dad say something?" Tasha asked, confounded. "Did he think this was something that would go unnoticed?"

"Well, it seems it did," Nora interjected with ill-timed humor, and received a quelling look from Natalie.

"I don't know," Natalie answered heavily. "I honestly don't have a clue. And I should have. God, how could I have missed this?"

"Hold on, it's not your fault." Tasha frowned, hating that Nat was ready to crucify herself. "*Dad* should've said something. It's not your job to parent our parents."

"Sage advice from the one who's never around," Nora said under her breath, but not quietly enough for Tasha to miss.

Tasha pointedly ignored that not-so-subtle dig and placed a hand on Natalie's shoulder, giving her a look that said *breathe,* before taking a breath herself to assess the damage. "It looks like a tree fell through it," she surmised, cocking her head to the side as she stepped into the room, looking for evidence to support her guess.

"Maybe a small pine or something during the last storm," Nora said, adding her two cents, then shook her head in annoyance. "Damn, it's just like Dad to hide something like this."

"Natalie, go find him. We'll get to the bottom of this and fix it," Tasha decided.

But Natalie was spared the effort as their father appeared in the hallway, and once he saw what they were staring at, his expression went from a man lost in a fog of his own grief to one who knew he was guilty.

Tasha expected bluster but he simply pursed his lips and said, "Close the door. You're letting in a draft." He turned around and shuffled toward the kitchen.

"A draft?" Tasha repeated, and was the first to follow. "*That* is not a draft. That—" she pointed toward the bedroom "—is a health hazard. There's a freaking hole in the wall! How long has this been like this?"

"What difference does it make?" their dad muttered, openly annoyed. "There's a hole and that's why the damn door was closed."

Tasha took one look at her sisters, who were

watching her closely with silent encouragement, and refused to back down. "Dad, why didn't you tell someone? You could've had someone come out and take a look, give you an estimate and have it fixed within a week or two. Was it like this when Mom was sick?"

He refused to answer.

"Dad? Was it like this when Mom was sick?" Tasha repeated.

"The door was shut and it was closed off. Besides, no one went in there, anyway," he answered defensively, his gaze darting from one daughter to the other. "I stuffed towels under the door and that kept out the draft. There's nothing to get yourself all worked up about."

Natalie joined the fray. "Dad, this is very serious. We have to get it fixed right away. This can't wait until spring."

He waved away her concern and started to walk away. "Leave it."

"That's not going to happen," Tasha called after him, his attitude percolating her own temper. "We're going to get it fixed whether you like it or not."

"Tasha." Natalie tugged at Tasha's sleeve with a frown. "That's not the best way to get him to agree."

"I don't care. That hole is a structural hazard to the rest of the house. It has to be fixed." Stubborn old man. Probably would've let the house fall down around his ears if they hadn't stumbled upon it. She huffed a sharp breath and turned to her sisters. "So, who are we going to find to fix this?" she asked, glancing back in the direction of the damage.

"The best handyman in the area kicked the bucket a few months back, and I wouldn't trust his son to build a doghouse, much less repair a gaping hole," Nora said.

"Well, that's easy…the Halvorsens, of course," Natalie said. "I don't think in Dad's current state of mind he'd let anyone else into the house."

"I don't know," Tasha said, shaking her head, not thrilled with the idea. "I'm sure there must be someone else."

"What's wrong with Josh?" Natalie asked, immediately warming to the idea. "He's working with his brothers at Halvorsen Construction. I'll bet he might even offer us a discount given the circumstances."

"That wouldn't be right," Tasha argued. "He has a son to provide for. If we were to hire him we'd pay him the going wage."

"Don't worry about that," Nora said. "Dean and Sammy will help us out. Besides, with the winter, they're probably a little slow. They'd more than likely welcome the work."

Natalie agreed. "Can you call him? Ask him to come out and give us an estimate?"

"Why can't one of you ask? Josh and I aren't close anymore," Tasha said, shifting uncomfortably. "It's not like we call each other up to chat."

"True, but I have errands to run this morning before I head to the bookstore, and Nora is going to take Dad to his doctor's appointment."

"What's wrong with Dad?" Tasha asked sharply.

"His blood pressure," Nora answered. "He refuses to eat right, but at least he takes his medication now and again, and with the stress of Mom passing, his doctor wants to make sure he's taking the right dosage."

Tasha nodded and tried to understand that circumstances had prevented her from knowing what happened with her family on a routine basis, but hated that she'd been kept out of the loop as far as their dad's health concerns.

"So, that leaves you to make the arrangements," Nora finished.

"Fine," Tasha groused, giving each sister a dark look. "But I want to go on record as saying that I think you guys are doing this on purpose in some misguided attempt to put Josh and me together, and if that's the case, it's juvenile and not going to work. This is bound to just make things even more awkward between us."

"Are you finished?" Natalie asked, some of her old spirit returning. When Tasha gave a short nod, she continued with a touch of irritation. "Stop thinking everything is about you. Halvorsen Construction is run by good, honest people we've known our entire lives. I know they'll do a good job of patching the wall and they won't overcharge. You and Josh will just have to find a way to get past your…well…past." She paused to grab her keys and met Tasha's humbled gaze. "And, you seemed to get along just fine at the wake. In fact, you two headed off into the sitting room, away from everyone else."

Tasha sputtered and her cheeks pinked. "There was nowhere to sit and the sitting room was empty!"

Natalie waved away Tasha's heated excuse and grabbed her keys. "I have to get going. Evan's at the store with Colton and they've probably destroyed everything at ground level. Can I trust you to call Josh as soon as possible?" she asked.

Tasha pressed her lips together but nodded.

"Good," she said, then turned to Nora, who'd watched the scene with speculative interest. "Tonight, you're on Dad detail." When she tried to protest, Natalie held her hand up. "Nope. It's you, sis. Tonight I'm going on a date with Evan and we've already arranged for a sitter. Nothing, and I mean nothing is getting in my way of spending some time with my husband. Got it?"

"Things okay with you and Evan?" Nora asked, and Tasha held her breath, knowing their mom's death had probably put a strain on everyone—a new marriage in particular.

Natalie grabbed her purse and answered resolutely, "They will be," before walking out the door, leaving Tasha and Nora to stare after her.

As bitchy as Nora could be, she was perceptive.

"Don't worry about them," she said. "I've never seen two people more in love with each other. It's kinda gross and mushy if you ask me." She slid a glance at Tasha. "Reminds me of you and Josh when I was a kid. You guys were pretty gross, too."

Tasha tried to brush off Nora's observation, but the blush warming her cheeks was too telling. Nora chuckled. "Don't forget to call lover-boy," she said before sauntering from the room, leaving Tasha to wonder angrily why everyone thought just because she and Josh shared something special in the past that they had any hope—or desire—to see it happen again.

She pressed the back of her hand to one cheek, felt the heat there and quickly dropped it to her side.

They were wrong. All of them. No matter what they think they see, Tasha thought with a touch of sadness. As far as Tasha was concerned, the past was dead.

JOSH WAS IN THE MIDDLE of refinishing his own kitchen cabinets when the cell phone hanging on his tool belt buzzed at his hip. The number didn't register on caller ID but it seemed vaguely familiar.

"Yeah, Josh here," he answered, pausing to wipe the grime from his forehead. The cabinets were old but they were solid, and it gave him something to do on his downtime.

"Josh, this is Tasha. Do you have a minute?"

"Uh, sure," he answered cautiously, surprised to hear her voice on the other end. "What do you need?"

"It's my dad. He…well, apparently forgot to mention to anyone that he had a huge, gaping hole in his hobby room from a tree crashing through the south wall during the last big storm, and, well, we need someone who can, um, fix it."

"Wow. A hole?"

"Complete with duct tape and plastic sheeting."

He rubbed his chin, speculating on the damage. "How big?"

She sighed. "Big enough to poke your head through and possibly step out to what used to be my mom's garden."

He whistled. That was pretty big. "You want me to ask Dean if he can send someone out?"

A sound of relief at his understanding followed. "Would you mind?"

"No, it's fine. Your dad can't go the whole winter with a hole in his house."

"Yeah, tell that to my dad. He's being his usual ornery self. He doesn't want us to fix it."

"Why not?"

She sighed. "I don't know. He probably didn't want a bunch of people in the house with mom in her final stages, which I can understand to a point, but it's really a hazard. Now he's just being difficult. You know how he can be."

"He's a tough old coot, that's for sure," he murmured in agreement, remembering the time Gerald

Simmons had caught him and Tasha kissing behind the house. Tasha had been sixteen with a body full enough to make him forget his own name. Her cutoff jeans were faded and worn, but as his hand had inched south to caress a handful of that curvaceous flesh, who'd come around the corner but Gerald himself, flashing indignant fire from his eyes and swearing that he was going to plumb cut that hand off if Josh didn't turn his daughter loose and get the hell off his property. A grin threatened at the corners of his mouth at the memory. He'd thought for sure the old man was going to take his head off. "All right, I'll be in touch."

"Thanks, Josh."

"Don't mention it," he finished, squelching the tingles in his gut at the prospect of seeing her on a regular basis. He didn't consider himself a glutton for punishment, so why couldn't he just push Tasha out of his head like he should?

Hefting his sander to return to his work, he heard the front door open, and expecting to see only his son, was surprised and dismayed to see that Carrie had followed Christopher into the house as if she had the right to do so. Gritting his teeth against the urge to remind her that she no longer had those kinds of privileges, he was derailed by the look on his son's face.

Chris stalked past him, heading straight for his bedroom, and he sighed heavily. "What happened?" he asked, directing his question at his ex-wife.

"Why do you look at me like that? Like I'm this horrible person? I'm just trying to find some way to break him out of his shell." She took a defensive posture, continuing, "You might think it's okay for him to live in his room, playing on the computer, but I think it's unhealthy. Life is about more than just games. He needs to socialize more."

"I don't think you have any right to pass judgment when you've skipped out on your visitation for the past few weekends. And for your information, he doesn't spend all day on the computer when he's with me," he answered, trying for patience, but he was fast losing his grip. "So, are you going to tell me what happened or do I have to play Twenty Questions?"

Carrie's expression reddened from Josh's abrupt demeanor, but she answered in a clipped tone. "I enrolled him in the Junior Golf League at the country club. Robert has a membership and suggested this might be a good way to get him involved in something." At his incredulous look, she slapped her thigh in frustration. "For crying out loud, Josh, it's *golf,* how hard can it be? You hit a ball and chase after it. I hardly even consider golf a sport." She looked away with a disappointed sigh. "But, apparently, golf isn't his thing, either. It was an abysmal day," she admitted, turning back to him, the blue of her eyes hardening. "And I blame you."

"Excuse me? I'm not the one who keeps trying to make him into something he's not," he said, struggling to remember that he didn't have to listen to this crap anymore. He drew a deep breath before continuing in the hopes that this conversation was reaching its end. "Instead of spending so much time and money on activities that Christopher is guaranteed to hate, why not try to get to know him? Here's a clue. He's not into sports, no matter how hard you push them."

She stiffened. "You think you know our son better than me? His own mother? I beg to differ." When he said nothing in response, only shrugged, her lip trembled with the force of her anger. "Perhaps if you weren't so busy trying to be his friend you'd see that you're not doing him any good as a father! Moving him from one school to another just because of one incident—"

"One incident?" he cut in, disbelief coloring his tone. "He could've been killed!"

"See? This is the problem. You've exaggerated what happened until it's so big the only thing Christopher could do was run away. Is that what you're trying to teach him, Josh? When there's a problem just run away? It's what you did our entire marriage, but I'd hoped you wouldn't want your son to follow in your footsteps."

"Carrie, you have ten seconds to get your ass out of my house," he said from between clenched teeth. Never in his life had he ever raised a hand against a woman, but right now, his hands were shaking from his desire to slap her silly. "Get out before I throw you out."

Carrie visibly paled at the threat she read in his eyes and took a faltering step backward as if not quite sure how to make an exit with her dignity intact. Finally, she lifted her chin and met his glare, though she scaled down her cutting tone. "I'm just trying to help him. Can you say the same?"

He pointed toward the door. "Out."

She sent one final angry stare his way and stiffly left, clacking down the porch steps in her ridiculous heels to climb into her sleek Mercedes. He didn't bother to watch her drive away, content with the sound of her retreating tires. Pushing his hand through his hair, he let out a short breath and stared up at the ceiling while he willed his blood pressure to come down to a healthy level. What a crock of shit. She didn't know jack about what was good for Christopher. If she did, she wouldn't keep forcing him to be someone he wasn't. It didn't matter how many baseball camps or soccer tryouts she sent him to, he wouldn't come out a jock. He just wasn't cut out for that.

Walking to Christopher's door, he pushed it open and peeked inside. "You okay?" he asked, only a little surprised to see Christopher was already online simultaneously chatting and logging onto his MySpace account. So the kid liked the Internet. Where was the harm in that? At least he knew where his kid was each night, unlike some parents. "You hungry?"

"Mom picked up McDonald's on the way," he answered without taking his eyes off the screen or his fingers from the keyboard. "Thanks, though."

Josh smiled. And the kid had manners, too. "Not too late, okay, buddy?"

"Yeah, sure, Dad."

Josh closed the door, wondering—only because of the seed Carrie had planted with her poisonous accusations—if Chris was acknowledging him or just blowing him off. No, he and Chris didn't have that kind of relationship. He shrugged off the lingering effect of Carrie's claim and returned to his sanding, content that everything was fine with the Halvorsen men.

CHAPTER SEVEN

"DEAN CALLED LAST NIGHT, said they'd come over sometime today to look at the damage," Tasha explained to her sisters the next morning over coffee.

"Oh, good." Natalie visibly relaxed. "I didn't sleep very well last night because I was worried about that damn hole."

"It's going to be fine," Nora said, between mouthfuls of blueberry scone. "Like I said, Dean and Sammy will fix us up. I wasn't worried."

Annoyed, Natalie glared at Nora. "Glad to hear you slept like a baby."

"So, when's he coming?" Nora asked, ignoring Natalie.

"He didn't say, just sometime today," Tasha answered. "I figured while we were waiting we could go through Mom's things."

"What's the rush?" Nora asked.

"No rush, exactly, but why wait?" Tasha countered, but she caught the knowing look in Natalie's eyes and averted her own. That was the disadvantage to sisters; they saw through your bullshit. "Well, I can't stay forever, and if you want my help we need to get moving," she said, dusting pastry from her hands until she caught Nora's hard look. *For crying out loud...* Tasha threw her hands up in exasperation. "What, Nora? What now?"

Nora's eyes cooled despite the anger radiating from her small frame. She stiffened, saying, "I find it insulting that you are so eager to hightail it out of here when we need you. Fine. You want to dig through Mom's things so badly, go ahead. Do it yourself."

Natalie moved to intervene, but Tasha could only glare, her own temper spiking at Nora's attitude.

"Nora, be fair..." Natalie's frustration was evident in her tone.

Nora made a small sound of disgust. "I have to meet a client about some landscaping. Thanks for the scone," she said.

Irritation washed over Tasha when she'd thought they'd heard the last of Nora's tirade, only to see Nora turn at the door.

"Just get over yourself already," Nora said. Tasha

sputtered indignantly, but Nora didn't give her the chance to say anything in her defense. "I get that there's something you guys aren't telling me about the reason why Tasha doesn't want to be here, but if you're not going to clue me in, you can't expect my sympathy…or understanding."

Tasha was too angry to listen to the logic in her sister's declaration. Several minutes passed before Tasha could speak again without wanting to rail at her youngest sister. "I don't know how much more of her crap I can take."

"You should tell her," Natalie said quietly. "She's not a kid anymore. And, she's right, until she knows why you're so reluctant, her attitude is not likely to change."

"Forgive me if I don't feel like shouting it from the rooftops," Tasha returned stonily. Natalie's take on the subject left Tasha feeling betrayed. "Besides, it's none of her business."

Natalie sighed and stared into her coffee cup as if searching for the right way to phrase her next statement. She lifted her gaze. "You're right…it's your business and no one else's but…Nora is your sister, too. And she loves you. Give her a chance."

"No." Tasha sent Natalie a firm look. "And I don't

want to talk about it anymore. I'll be in Mom's side of the closet pulling her clothes if you need me."

Tasha left the room before Natalie could say anything, anger fueling her steps until she was standing before her mother's closet, breathing in short, tight huffs.

She ran her tongue across lips chapped from dehydration, her mind spinning from her conversation with her sisters. Determined to focus on something other than her acidic stomach, she pushed open the closet door and staggered at the faint, beguiling scent of Chanel that followed.

Mom.

Tasha inhaled deeply with closed eyes and let the scent roll over her in a comforting wave. Missy had always been the gentle, guiding force that kept the girls' willful personalities from colliding into one another. Without her, there was nothing to keep their worst qualities from taking over during a weak moment. Tears stung her eyes and she drifted through a handful of memories.

Mom in her garden, knees dirt-stained, dragging bags of mulch to the churned topsoil and grinning as she brought a basket of fresh cucumbers, tomatoes and peppers from her glorious, well-tended garden.

Mom in the kitchen, flour dusting the apron tied around her slim waist and a wealth of love shining from her eyes as she listened to her girls chatter about their school day.

Mom in her favorite chair, nodding off with a magazine sliding from her slack fingers while Dad watched reruns of *The Honeymooners.*

Tasha sank to the bed and dropped her face into her palms, shaking as her heart poured out its never-ending grief. She mourned the loss of a mother as only a daughter can. An hour later, she jerked at the strong, male voice at her back.

"Tasha? You okay?"

"Sammy?" Josh's younger brother stood in the doorway, his face breaking into a wide grin as she quickly wiped at her wet cheeks and rushed to accept a bear hug from an only slightly shorter version of Josh. "Sammy…I hardly recognized you! You're all grown up," she said, drawing away so she could regard him more closely. "The last time I saw you, you were only sixteen, same as Nora. What have you been up to?"

"Working with Dean. In fact, he sent me over here to take a look at the hole Josh was talking about."

As if remembering, she groaned and pointed.

"Oh, yeah…it's in what used to be Natalie's room. Come on, I'll show you."

Stepping into the hallway, she called out to Natalie but was met with silence. Sammy answered instead.

"We passed each other on the way. It looked like she had your Dad in the car with her. Should I come back later?"

"No, no, of course not." Tasha felt bad for snapping at Natalie but hid her consternation from Sammy. She opened the door and allowed it to swing wide. "As you can see, it's pretty big. I still can't believe nobody knew about it."

Sammy's eyes widened at the destruction, but he was also holding back a laugh. Sammy inherited the Halvorsen sense of humor. Sammy laughed at everything. "How'd this happen?"

"Who knows? Like I told Josh on the phone, it was likely caused by a tree from the last storm, but it's just an educated guess. What do you think?"

"I think it's a fair guess," he said, moving to the plastic sheeting and pulling it from the hole. He peered down, then up, surveying the damage with a critical eye. It was an odd thing to be standing there with a grown-up Sammy when she'd left behind a kid. Now he was going to help fix their wall.

"Shouldn't be too hard to patch, probably only take a week to fix. Structurally, it seems sound, but I'll have Dean come out to make sure. He'll also be able to give you an official estimate and time frame."

"Thanks, Sammy," Tasha said, her voice still a little nasal-sounding from her crying jag. He held the door open for her and then closed it behind them. Tasha was impressed. "When did you turn into a gentleman?" she asked playfully.

He grinned, but a blush gave away his embarrassment. "Somewhere along the way, I suppose. When'd you get even hotter than when you were going out with my dumb brother?"

"Sammy!" She laughed, gesturing for him to follow her into the kitchen. "Come share a scone with me."

"A scone? Do I look like the kind of guy who eats scones?" Sammy asked, but he was already eyeing the blueberry choice with a glint in his eye. He accepted the small plate with a wink. "Well, just for you."

"Thanks," Tasha returned dryly, enjoying the unexpected reunion. "Tell me what you've been up to," she demanded as she bit into her second scone of the day.

"I already told you, working with Dean. That's about the extent of it. Not everyone leads such an exotic life," Sammy teased, and she blushed. "The question I should be asking is what *you've* been up to all these years. I mean, I've heard all sorts of things."

"Like what?"

"Well, that you're saving some native tribe from the terrors of outdoor plumbing and creating a democracy for some other tribe deep in the jungle who don't even wear pants!"

"You don't need pants in the jungle," she pointed out, and Sammy acknowledged that small fact. Tasha smiled and continued, "And, I feel obligated to set the record straight, seeing as your source isn't very accurate. I haven't been involved in any democracy-making project, but I have helped create a sewage system, and currently I'm working with physicians from Punta Gorda who travel to an outpost in the Maya Mountains to help vaccinate or treat the villagers who won't come down to seek medical attention on their own. And, I just started with a team who's working on building a serviceable water-treatment plant for the small village."

"That's even better than the rumors," Sammy said, losing some of his jocularity until he crumpled his napkin into a ball and sent it flying in a perfect arc into the trash can. "So, are you staying here or going back to your glorious loincloth-wearing villagers?"

The way Sammy phrased it, it was hard not to giggle, though the question was not posed without seriousness and Tasha knew it. Sobering, she nodded. "I'm going back."

Disappointment washed over his strong face. "That's too bad. I was hoping you'd stay."

"Why? Thinking of asking me out on a date?"

"If Josh doesn't I just might."

Sadness replaced her former lightheartedness and she shook her head. "Sammy…Josh and I don't have a future beyond what we already shared in the past. It seems Josh and I are the only ones who realize that simple fact."

"Why?"

"Why what?"

"Why does it have to stay in the past?" Sammy asked.

She stared at him quizzically. "Because it does. C'mon, Sammy…where's this coming from?"

Sammy seemed caught and sheepishly shrugged his shoulders. "I dunno…I just see my brother hurting and you were always the one who could reach him."

"What's wrong with Josh? He seemed fine at the wake." That wasn't entirely true. There'd been sadness hiding in his eyes, but she suspected a divorce wasn't a picnic.

Sammy waved away her question, regret in his expression. "Forget I said anything. If Josh knew I'd said anything, he'd tear me a new one. It's good to see you again, Tasha…even if you're still out of my league."

He gave her another one of his signature Sammy grins, all boyish charm and roguish good looks, and Tasha wished Nora had seen Sammy as more than a friend once they were old enough to notice those kinds of things. She sighed and accepted another hug. It felt good to see Sammy.

Tasha saw Sammy to the door and waved as he drove away, but his last comment was still ringing in her head. She couldn't escape the thought that deep down, hidden from everyone, was a pain Josh was suffering alone.

And it bothered her more than it should.

CHAPTER EIGHT

Josh arrived at Gerald Simmons's house, ready to work but still griping at Dean for sending him instead of someone else on the crew. But his own grousing didn't compare to the silent anger written all over his son's face. Josh learned today was a pro day at school, which meant only the teachers went, giving the students a day off, and he'd hit upon the bright idea to have Christopher help him out at the job site.

Christopher had turned him down and immediately powered up his computers, the action bothering Josh more than he wanted to admit. And then, after trying to appeal to some sense of male bonding and failing, he flat out insisted Christopher come. Carrie might've been right about one small thing: the boy spent way too much time indoors.

So, his teenage son sat, sullen and uncommunicative, beside him, as they pulled up to the Simmonses' place.

He drew a deep breath and stared at the house, knowing Tasha was probably in there with one or both of her sisters. Running into Tasha before had been accidental; the wake carefully handled…but this? He wanted to kick his brother in the tender spots for his obvious attempt at throwing them together.

"I thought you said we were going to a job site?" Christopher asked, his annoyed expression marred by a subtle confusion.

"This is the job site. We're repairing the side of the house that was hit by a tree. The Simmons family are friends so they thought of Uncle Dean's construction company to repair it."

Christopher nodded but didn't lose his dour mood. Josh withheld a sigh and tried to remember that he hadn't always been a bowl of sunshine growing up, either.

He was just about to knock on the door when Nora appeared, looking hurried.

"Hey, Josh!" Nora said, bolting past him to her truck. She waved at the house and shouted from her window as she pulled out of the driveway. "Tasha and Nat are inside. Tell Sammy I said hi!"

Josh agreed by way of a wave and Christopher stared. "Who was that?" he asked.

"Nora Simmons, the youngest. She's a good friend of your uncle Sammy's. C'mon, let's get inside."

Knocking, he entered with his head first, looking for either the Simmons women or Gerald himself. Someone hollered for him to come on in and he closed the door behind Christopher and him.

Without Missy's comforting presence, the house seemed empty. If he felt it, he could only imagine how Tasha and her family felt.

Tasha and Natalie came from their parents' bedroom, each carrying a good-size box, and a stronger sense of sadness washed over him as he realized they were carrying Missy's things. One box was labeled Goodwill, the other Personal.

"Do you need some help?" he asked, needing to feel useful. "Me and Chris can load the Goodwill stuff in my truck and take it in for you."

Tasha's eyes were uncommonly bright with unshed tears, but she shook her head. "I'll do it," she said, moving past him to put the box against the wall where the rest would undoubtedly go. She added with a briefly held smile. "Thanks, though."

Josh pulled Christopher out in front of him to introduce him to Tasha. "This is my son, Christopher. Christopher, this is my friend Tasha."

Christopher extended his hand, and Josh was pleased to see even in a bad mood he didn't neglect his manners. "Nice to meet you," he mumbled.

"Nice to meet you, too," she said, her voice strained. She cast a look Josh's way and he was struck by how much raw emotion he saw. "He looks so much like you when you were a kid."

Josh smiled, knowing it was true. Christopher had Carrie's nose, but otherwise, he did look remarkably like Josh had at that age. He only hoped Christopher filled out like he had. "I brought him to help out since school was out for the day," he said.

She nodded her approval. "Like you and your brothers used to work with your dad. That's so great." Tasha gave Christopher a warm smile. "You're lucky to have such a talented father who's willing to teach you everything he knows. Being able to work with your hands will be useful when you're an adult."

Christopher shrugged but didn't look convinced. "If you say so."

"Well, I'd better get back to what I was doing.

Good to see you again, Josh…Christopher," she said, acknowledging his son, and then disappeared.

Natalie entered the room and detoured with a box to a separate area so as not to mix it with the ones leaving. She stretched her back as if she'd been bent over boxes the entire morning. "Can I get you some coffee?" she asked, twisting one way then another. "I've got decaf if you've already had a few cups."

Josh wouldn't mind a cup, but he was on the clock and declined. Plus, with Christopher in his current mood he didn't want to waste too much time. "Dean sent me to patch up that wall, so I think I'll just get to it."

"All work and no play makes Josh a dull boy," Natalie teased, though there were dark circles under her eyes. Missy's death was hard on them all.

"Where's your dad?" he asked.

Natalie sighed and pointed at the back porch. "He's taken to sitting there for hours at a time. It's all we can do to get him to eat now and then. But I've left him there for the time being because right now I don't think he's up to watching us divvy up Mom's things."

"That's wise," he agreed, though his gaze strayed to the porch. It wasn't healthy for the old man to sit outside in the dead of winter. Plus, it just wasn't like the Gerald Simmons he'd grown up with. "Maybe I should go talk to him."

"I don't know what you could say that we haven't already. Besides, he's not really himself right now. He might say something…well, for lack of a better word, rude, and I wouldn't want you to hold it against him."

He chuckled. "The Gerald I know was never interested in playing nice when it didn't suit him."

Natalie smiled. "You're right. Feel free, but don't say I didn't warn you."

"Fair enough." Moving toward the back porch, he paused. "On second thought, would you mind bringing two cups of coffee? Straight, no sugar for me and however your dad likes his. And maybe Christopher can lend you a hand for a few minutes?"

"You got it," Natalie said, and headed into the kitchen.

"Dad, I don't want to help out. I want to go home," Christopher complained when Natalie was out of earshot. "Let's just get started so we can leave. Some of us had plans that didn't include manual labor."

Disappointment washed over him at his son's attitude. "We're here and these ladies need some help. There's nothing at the house that can't wait until tonight. Besides, as far as I could tell you were just on your computer."

"Yeah, what's wrong with that?" Christopher said.

Josh tried to choose his words carefully, knowing how Carrie tended to berate their son for his computer habits. "Nothing is wrong with it in *moderation,* son. But you've exceeded moderation a long time ago. I'm not saying you have to give it up, but just give it a rest for a bit and try to get used to your new surroundings. What do you say?"

"Do I get a choice?"

Josh exhaled loudly, his patience thinning. "Chris—"

Natalie returned carrying two coffee mugs and Josh swallowed the rest of his lecture. Christopher wasn't in the mood to listen, anyway. He accepted the mugs with thanks.

"I don't know if it's going to make a difference, but I sure appreciate your effort," Natalie said honestly.

Josh watched Gerald as he sat staring at the trees lining his backyard, lost in thoughts only he could read.

"I'm happy to try," Josh said, and Natalie opened the door for him. He stepped outside with a steaming cup in each hand as Natalie commandeered his son.

Josh was standing right beside him before Gerald noticed, turning stiffly as if the cold had fused his joints together.

Josh held out the cup. "Just the way you like it. Natalie says so."

It took a moment, but soon Gerald's gaze cleared and he squinted. "What are you doing here?" he asked gruffly, but he accepted the mug.

"Your daughters hired Halvorsen Construction to fix that hole in Natalie's old room."

Gerald grunted. "Yeah, what's that got to do with you?"

"I'm working with Dean for a bit. Why are you sitting out here in the cold like a dumb fool?"

"Because I like it out here."

Right. He took a measured sip from his mug. "So, what can you tell me about that hole?"

"It's a hole, boy! What's it look like?" Gerald seemed flustered, his florid face turning pink in a flash. But his ire was short-lived, as if he didn't have the energy to sustain it. "I was going to fix it. Damn oak came right through the window. But I didn't want a bunch of strangers tromping through the house when Missy was so sick. She needed some peace. So I put up some plastic sheeting to keep out the rain and put towels under the doorway to keep out most of the draft. I was going to fix it, even placed a few calls to get an estimate, but then Missy took a turn for the worse and she had such a hard time sleeping because of the pain I wasn't about to have a lot of hammering going on when she was fighting for every bit of shut-eye she could get. It was the only thing I could do for her."

Josh nodded, understanding the man's need to protect his wife against the one thing he thought he could control.

Gerald blew out a short breath and it plumed in the cold air. "By the end, Missy was in so much pain they kept her pretty drugged from the morphine. I couldn't even think about that hole, and honestly, I didn't have to… No one seemed to notice until now. For Gemini's sake, it's only been two months since it happened. Everyone needs to just settle down."

"The girls are worried about it, though," Josh commented, and Gerald snorted lightly, which told Josh the old man thought they were overreacting. "You might've at least told Natalie. Tasha said she about had a nervous breakdown when she saw the damage."

At that, Gerald seemed to soften. "I didn't want to worry anyone. This house was full of enough pain and misery as it was," he added under his breath.

Josh took another sip, letting the silence slide between them. Gerald wasn't a man prone to whining or sharing, for that matter, but Josh suspected that the old man didn't know how to deal with his grief and that hole represented more than just a job that needed doing. If left up to Gerald, Josh had a good feeling it wouldn't get fixed for a long while. Tasha had been right to call. Finishing his coffee, he looked at Gerald. "You coming in?"

Gerald didn't answer, only lifted the mug to his blue lips and shrugged. "Why? There's nothing in that house for me anymore."

"There's nothing out here but pneumonia," Josh reminded him harshly. "Missy's gone. Sitting outside freezing your ass off isn't going to bring her back. Besides, you're scaring Natalie. It looks like she hasn't had a decent night's sleep in weeks. And Tasha… Well, she's hurting, too."

"They should just leave me alone," Gerald muttered.

"You know they won't."

The old man exhaled with frustration, but Josh wasn't in the mood to listen. Bitterness had curdled Gerald's grief until the old man was sniping at everyone who tried to help, his daughters included. Josh knew Tasha and her sisters didn't need to deal with Gerald in this manner on top of everything else. "No sense in making a bad situation worse. Isn't that what you used to tell me whenever I'd gotten into a scrap and tried hiding out here so my own dad didn't tan my hide?"

"That's different," Gerald mumbled.

"Good advice is good advice no matter who's giving it out, and right now you're acting like an old fool."

When Gerald only glared at him, Josh stood his ground. The old man was coming inside whether he liked it or not. "If you don't come inside right now, I'll leave you to the mercy of all three of your daughters. In their current mood, I wouldn't push it. As far as I can tell, none of them inherited Missy's gentle disposition."

Gerald seemed to mull over Josh's veiled threat, and when he finally stood, Josh figured the threat held merit. But even as Gerald tottered with uneven steps on stiffened limbs, he hadn't lost his sour attitude. "A man can't just grieve his own way without people sticking their noses where they don't belong," he said, shooting a dark look Josh's way.

Josh caught movement out of his peripheral vision and Tasha disappeared from behind the lace curtain of the porch side window. A strange, unwelcome fluttering erupted in his gut at the knowledge she'd been watching him with her father. Was he out of line for what he did? Josh wasn't sure. He was just doing what he felt was right for a man he'd known his entire life. Josh sighed and followed Gerald into the house. At least the old man wasn't sitting outside anymore, even if he was grousing at the interference.

Tasha paused at her parents' bedroom and met his gaze. Something flickered in her stare that looked similar to gratitude but was flavored with something deeper, and he could feel the magnitude of her emotion as strongly as if she'd physically touched him. A small smile lifted the corner of her generous mouth, and he acknowledged their unspoken conversation with a slight nod. Tasha disappeared and the door closed.

LATER THAT NIGHT, TASHA sat with Natalie in the darkened living room, both exhausted from the emotional day.

"Dad finally go to bed?" Tasha asked.

"Yeah."

"Good."

"I've been thinking," Natalie started, then

swiveled her head to regard Tasha. "Someday you're going to need to talk to Dad about…that day."

Tasha grimaced with irritation. Why was Natalie always pushing the issue? She met her sister's stare. "And why is that?"

"Because it's an open wound between you two. And I think this family is suffering enough without dragging around old baggage."

Tasha sighed in spite of herself. She'd often rehearsed what she might say to her father if she ever found the courage, but the timing never seemed right. Then, after enough years had gone by, she figured it was best not to bring up old arguments. "Just let it go, Nat."

But Natalie wouldn't. "I think that's a mistake."

"I don't really care what you think right now. It's my decision and I don't feel like sharing or opening up something I've done my best to put behind me. Sometimes I regret telling *you.*"

The last part was muttered, but Natalie had perfect hearing. Tasha regretted her comment, but it was out there and she couldn't take it back. *Crap.* "I'm sorry. I shouldn't have said that. I'm just worn out from the day."

Natalie nodded, but when she rose, her movements were rigid. "I have to get home. I have to be at the bookstore tomorrow and Nora is busy with a new client. That leaves you to help Dad with Josh. Sorry," she added with little sincerity, eyes glittering with unshed tears. "But sometimes we end up with jobs that suck."

Such as carrying the burden of your sister's secret. That's what she didn't say, and Tasha knew it.

CHAPTER NINE

THE NEXT FEW DAYS WERE surreal. At first, Tasha was jarred each time she saw Josh round the corner as he went to and from his work truck to get parts or tools, but oddly, it was soothing to have him there. They didn't go out of their way to speak to each other but his presence was a privately welcomed one.

Natalie and Nora had convinced their father to join a support group at the senior center, though Tasha wasn't sure how they did it. She suspected Natalie had cajoled him while Nora had bullied him until he agreed just to escape them both. An unexpected giggle popped from her mouth and she looked around guiltily. It didn't seem right to laugh when her mom had only just died. Weary from packing up more personal items, Tasha went to the kitchen for a cup of coffee to bolster her flagging reserve. Cup in hand, she passed by her father's hobby room. Josh had put up a thick plastic sheet over the doorway to minimize the draft coming from the room while he fixed the damage, but Tasha could see his blurred outline as he worked.

Josh had pulled the demolished siding, drywall and window framing from the house and he was checking the studs for structural damage. Shivering from the cold coming from just the sheet, she wondered how Josh withstood the extreme temperature in the room. He was dressed warmly but not overly so, and there was a small space heater inside but it didn't take away the chill. Her hands curled around the mug for its warmth, and she wondered if he was going to break for lunch or keep working.

A thought occurred to her and she returned to the kitchen.

JOSH COULDN'T FEEL HIS fingers anymore. Pulling his work gloves from his hands, he walked to the space heater and tried warming them. It wasn't ideal to make a repair like this in the dead of winter, but it wouldn't have waited until spring. Feeling returned to his fingers in a rush of tingling pain and he replaced his gloves. He'd just picked up his drill again when Tasha pushed aside the plastic sheeting and crooked her finger at him.

"Take a break," she suggested, and disappeared.

Josh hadn't planned to stop unnecessarily—he'd even forgone bringing a lunch—but curiosity got the better of him.

He set down his drill and followed, closing the door behind him.

Savory smells and warmth wafted from the kitchen and Josh's stomach growled. He rubbed at his gut with the realization that skipping lunch wasn't such a hot idea. Now hunger overruled his good sense. He entered the kitchen and Tasha turned with a shy smile. "I made you some soup to warm you up," she explained, motioning for him to take a seat at the island counter.

Josh went to do as she directed when he caught sight of his hands. Grimacing and wondering at his manners, he detoured to the sink. "Smells good," he said as he scrubbed the dust and dirt from his callused hands. "What is it?"

"Nothing fancy, really. Just good old-fashioned creamy chicken soup with a little cheese tortellini thrown in. I made some garlic bread to go with it, too." His stomach growled again and Tasha grinned. "Good thing I made extra."

Josh tried to smother the grin he felt coming, knowing full well he shouldn't accept her offer, but his mouth was already anticipating a mouthful of what she was ladling into a bowl. "Need help?" he asked.

"Nope. Just take a seat."

He did as she requested and Tasha placed a steaming bowl in front of him before returning to pull the bread from the oven. He accepted two slices and waited for Tasha.

Sliding beside him, Tasha flashed him a smile for the courtesy and motioned for him to dig in.

"Pretty good," he admitted around mouthfuls. He sent an inquisitive glance her way. "Where'd you learn to cook like this?"

Tasha shrugged. "Here and there. Living at the outposts over the years, I've picked up frugal cooking methods. Here in the States, there's so much waste. In developing countries, you learn how to make the best use of spices, garlic or whatever leftovers you have at hand. Natalie has stocked Dad's pantry with more food than he'll ever need, but she wants to make sure he eats."

"Your dad's really taking this hard, isn't he?" It was a rhetorical question. He'd seen the devastation in the man firsthand but he sensed Tasha was holding a lot inside. He sensed a lot with Tasha. It made him squirm and yearn for more at the same time. He'd always considered himself a simple man; but at the moment he felt damn complicated.

Tasha stirred her soup slowly, ostensibly to cool it, but Josh knew she was mulling over her answer. When she finally spoke again, her brow was troubled. "My dad…doesn't know how to live without Mom. She did everything for him. It was the way their relationship worked. He was the gruff disciplinarian; she was the heart. He brought home the money and she ran the house. I think my dad doesn't know how to be without his counterpart. She was…a part of him." She looked at him, her gaze soft and a little lost. "I know how he feels. I still can't believe she's gone."

Josh nodded but remained silent. Words in this particular instance were useless, and he was never the kind of man to fill silence with the sound of his own voice. His parents were still alive; he could only imagine the heartache Tasha and her family were going through.

"That's how most families around here are," he answered. "Emmett's Mill is as traditional as they come."

"Yeah, well, maybe if my mom had put a little responsibility on my dad for the house he wouldn't be so lost without her now."

"It doesn't work that way."

She stared. "What do you mean?"

"Your parents were comfortable with their roles. Can you see your dad trying to balance a checkbook or cruising the aisles at the grocery store? On the flip side, could you see your mom mowing the lawn or chopping wood?"

Tasha offered a short-lived smile to indicate she understood where he was going, then sighed. "I know, but now…he's a shell of the man he was without her. I can't stay here forever. What's going to happen when I leave?"

"Don't think about that right now. Focus on what has to be done this moment." *That's what I do*. Thinking too hard about the future was overwhelming…especially when you're starting from scratch.

"I guess."

Tasha returned to her soup and Josh did the same. Several minutes passed before Tasha spoke again.

"I hope Christopher is adjusting," she offered. "I imagine transferring to another high school is rough on a kid, especially when they don't know anyone."

"He knows Brandon, Dean's son," Josh said, wincing privately at the touch of defense in his tone. Despite the incident at school, Josh was still questioning whether it was the right decision to move Christopher away from everyone he knew. His son hadn't been happy, but Josh had made an executive decision. And, he had to stick with it. "Besides, our alma mater is better than his last high school. A prison yard would be better," he added darkly.

Tasha startled. "What do you mean?"

"Nothing, forget I said anything," he said, moving away from the counter. "Thanks for lunch."

"Josh, wait," Tasha called after him, and he cursed his mouth. He stopped just before the entryway and Tasha caught up to him. The open concern shining in her eyes made him wish things were different between them. A private part of himself wanted to lean on her as a friend, but it was a selfish desire that he wouldn't entertain. Tasha had enough on her plate without his problems. "What's bothering you? Did something bad happen at Christopher's last school?"

Josh answered with heavy silence, a war waging in his mind as he contemplated his answer. The long months of struggling alone with Christopher's academic woes, as well as the crushing weight of his failed marriage, were working against him as he realized he wanted to tell Tasha.

"He was bullied pretty bad," Josh finally admitted. "Some punks…they were going to cut him." Tasha's gasp spurred him on and the words came out in a tumble. "They cornered Christopher at lunch in an area that didn't have a security camera or a campus cop around. He was fine," he added, his tone almost more of a reassurance to himself than for the sake of his explanation. "He was lucky."

"Oh, my goodness…" she breathed, her hand going to her mouth. "That's awful."

He shook his head. "I figured it was just going to get worse and I didn't want to bury my only kid just because some punk didn't like the way he looked."

"You did the right thing," she said resolutely, surprising him. "You did exactly what I would've done in your shoes." His reaction made her cock her head at him. "What? Just because I don't have kids of my own doesn't mean I can't empathize? Did you file a police report?"

Respect for her logical train of thought made him nod. "Of course, but because there wasn't any actual physical contact, it's just a misdemeanor and even that charge probably won't stick. I figured it was best to just get the hell out of Dodge. Stockton was never my choice, anyway."

Too revealing, he thought, but somehow the gate had been pried open a few inches and his guard was down. It had always been that way with Tasha. "I'd better get back to work," he said, moving to the door. Her voice, soft and hesitant, stopped him.

"Did you love her?"

Josh paused, then met her gaze, knowing she'd see the truth no matter what he said. "Yes. I did." He offered a pained smile. "Crazy, huh?"

She swallowed and shook her head slowly. "No. Not at all. I'm glad. Everyone deserves love, Josh."

He didn't know what to say to that. His marriage to Carrie was a failure of the first rate. He'd tried; they'd both tried, he supposed. But some things weren't meant to last. Tasha, of all people, probably knew that better than most.

CHRISTOPHER GLANCED AT the digital clock on his dresser. He had another hour before his dad got home. Logging off his Yahoo Messenger, Christopher straightened and pulled a set of codes he'd gotten from his friend OgDog from his bottom drawer. Og was a gamer, like him, but he'd recently hacked into the main-

frame of Zodiac Games, the creator of his and Og's
favorite game, Zenith Rising. Everyone in the gaming
world knew that Zodiac was testing the sequel to Zenith
Rising in select cities under an umbrella of secrecy.
Gaming espionage was big business and OgDog hit the
jackpot when he managed to lift the codes. He'd been
itching to hack into Zodiac since OgDog IM'ed him
to tell him they worked. Then, his mom had shown
up—of all the times for her to go all maternal—and
he'd had to shelve his plans until he got back.

But then he'd chickened out. He was shaking
with anticipation, but there was a healthy dose of
trepidation, too. What if he got caught? Could he go
to jail? Prison? Christopher had trouble swallowing
at the thought.

His gaze strayed to the small bit of paper where
the codes beckoned, and sweat popped along his
brow. What was the point of having them if he wasn't
going to use them? Og would tease him mercilessly,
and rightly so. If Christopher learned Og was sitting
on a virtual gold mine like that, he'd never let him
live it down.

Biting down on his lip, he logged back onto Yahoo
and IM'ed Og.

Hellkaracks: You sure they work?
OgDog: Dude! You still haven't used them?

Christopher shifted in his chair under his friend's virtual rebuke.

Hellkaracks: I haven't had the chance. Mom showed up. Had to go.
OgDog: You don't know what you're missing, dude. It rocks.
Hellkaracks: It is as good as Zenith?
OgDog: Find out yourself.

OgDog logged off and Christopher followed. He picked up the codes and stared at the innocuous set of numbers. It was almost criminal *not* to try them out. Drawing a deep breath, he rolled to his Linux computer and let it boot.

CHAPTER TEN

BY THE TIME JOSH GOT HOME, he was exhausted. It wasn't just his hard day's work—he was emotionally spent. Being around Tasha was harder than he imagined it would be.

Rounding the corner, he simultaneously knocked and opened Christopher's door.

His son jumped at the intrusion, but Josh was more interested in the darkened room. "What are you doing sitting in the dark, Chris?" he asked, flipping the light and watching in amusement as Christopher shrank from the brightness. "Done your homework yet?"

"Yeah," Christopher answered, rubbing at his eyes. "What's for dinner?"

"I brought home some soup my friend Tasha made today. It's really good. I'll have it warmed up in five."

Christopher made a noncommittal noise that Josh

didn't care for, and Josh snapped his fingers at his son. "You. Dinner. Now."

"All right, Dad. I'll be there in a minute."

Josh nodded and moved toward the door. Turning, he gestured to the computer. "What are you working on?"

Christopher shrugged but powered down. "Nothing special. Just goofing around."

"You're not doing anything illegal, right?" Josh joked, and Christopher's eyes widened in an instant, making Josh a little uneasy until Christopher shook his head. Josh breathed a secret sigh of relief against his intuition ringing warning bells. It was Carrie's fault. She had his head all turned around. Christopher wouldn't do anything illegal, he thought. He was a good kid.

Josh was halfway to the kitchen when there was a knock at the front door. Detouring, he opened it to find his little brother, Sammy, blowing on his fingers and stamping his feet. "You gonna ask me in or keep me outside freezing my ass off?" he teased, breaking into a wide grin that was almost infectious.

"What's up, little brother?" Josh asked, closing the door behind Sammy. "Hungry? I was about to put on some soup."

"Soup? You really know how to entertain. Campbell's? Or that fancy stuff by Wolfgang Puck? I've got a finicky palette, you know."

Josh snorted as he headed toward the kitchen. "This coming from the man who used to think his boogers were a delicacy."

"Hey! No fair. I'm sure you did your share of disgusting childhood things. I'll have to ask Dean to get the scoop on you."

Josh put the soup on the stove. "Is that what you're here for? Childhood dirt? If that's the case, you're out of luck…I was a saint."

Sammy laughed out loud. "Yeah…right. Damn, that smells good. Maybe I will have some."

Josh smiled and grabbed a bowl. He hollered for Christopher and ladled some of Tasha's soup into a bowl for Sammy. "So you were saying? What's the occasion for the visit?"

"Just thought I'd come by and see how you're doing with that reconstruction job over at the Simmonses' place. Seeing as it's not really your forte, being a welder by trade. Wanted to make sure the wall wasn't going to cave in with the first strong wind."

Josh chuckled. "Is that so? Well, don't strain your little brain. The Simmons job isn't the first construction job I've taken on. I used to work with Dad, too, you know."

"Yeah, yeah, but your memory isn't what it used to be."

"What are you talking about?"

"I mean, if you had any inkling how amazing, not to mention beautiful, Tasha Simmons was and still is, you'd never have let her slip through your fingers."

All good humor fled as he stared at his little brother. "Drop it, Sam."

But Sammy wasn't deterred. "Listen, I know you're hurting because of Carrie, but you two never had the chemistry you and Tasha shared. I was just a kid, but even I could see there was something special there."

"You've seen too many movies."

"Maybe," Sammy agreed with a grin, not the least bit put off by the dark glower Josh was sending his way. "But where's the harm in rekindling a little something?"

Josh didn't want to use Tasha in that way. He was hurting inside. Anything he allowed to spark to life would only be transient and Tasha deserved better. He preferred to cherish his memories, rather than taint them for selfish purposes. Ignoring Sammy, he grabbed a bowl and ladled himself some soup.

Sammy grabbed his own bowl and followed Josh into the living room. "What's the big deal? You like her, she likes you—"

"What are you talking about?" he asked sharply, eyeing his brother. "When did you talk to Tasha?"

The delighted look on Sammy's face made Josh want to rearrange it. "Someone's sensitive, aren't they?" Sammy said, giving Josh a sly look.

Josh made a disgusted sound, but inside an uncomfortable twinge told him Sammy knew a bit too much about his older brother. "Eat your damn soup and go home," he said sourly.

Christopher walked by with his bowl of soup in the direction of his room when Josh asked him to eat with them. Christopher stopped, but it was clear by his expression that he'd rather not. "Dad, I've got homework."

"You said it was all done," Josh said, frowning when Christopher shrugged as if that information wasn't relevant.

"I forgot about some stuff," Christopher answered.

"All right. I guess you'd better get it done," Josh said with a sigh. "Make sure you put your bowl away when you're done. We don't need ants."

"Okay, okay," Christopher said, and disappeared.

Josh bent to return to his soup until he realized Sammy was regarding him seriously. That in itself was enough to give him pause. He narrowed his gaze at his brother. "What's on your mind now?"

"Everything okay with Chris?"

"Yeah, why?"

"He seems a little…preoccupied."

"What teenager isn't?" Josh snorted, but lately, he'd been harboring some concerns himself. Josh chalked Christopher's withdrawal up to the stress of moving and Carrie's flighty parental excursions; he assumed Christopher would get through it in his own time. He sighed in spite of himself. "He's having a difficult time with things. The move… Carrie…you know."

Sammy nodded. "I figured. Still, you might want to keep an eye on him. He's starting to turn into one of those trench-coat mafia types. Next thing you know, he'll be building a bomb in the garage."

"Not hardly," Josh retorted. "Christopher's not the type."

"I hope not. Brandon still helping him out at school?" Sammy asked. Brandon was a good kid. Straight A's, popular and athletic. In fact, except for the grades, Brandon was a lot like Josh had been in school. Sometimes he wondered how his nephew ended up with his share of DNA.

"I don't know," Josh admitted. "I hope so. But I'm not sure."

Again, Sammy nodded, his expression grave—which was an odd fit for his younger brother. "Me, too... Hey, if you need someone to talk to him, I'm willing to take him under my wing."

"That's a scary thought," Josh muttered, but there was no rancor in it. He appreciated his brothers' help, even if it felt a little intrusive at times. He looked to Sammy. "Thanks, little brother."

"No problem. Now, about Tasha..."

TASHA BIT HER LIP as she lifted an old journal from a box of her childhood things. The years melted away as she held the warped notebook in her hands. Senior year. Emmett's Mill High, home of the Grizzlies.

Light filtered from the small attic window and sent wan shafts of sunlight into the cold, cluttered room. Dust motes danced before her eyes and her fingers lightly traced the faded lettering on the plain diary. She didn't feel the cold seeping into her bones, nor did she listen to the voice in her head that directed her to return it to the box. She'd come up here to put away her mom's things, not lose herself in high-school memories.

Still…her fingers disobeyed her brain and soon she was opening the first page.

As she read the first entry, a smile warmed her mouth. She'd been so full of life. Unstoppable, in her mind. Tasha flipped through a few more pages. Cheerleading, the winter formal, who was dating who and Josh. Lots of stuff about Josh.

A wistful sigh escaped as she read one particular entry.

Josh and I have a special night planned. I told Mom I'm staying at Hannah's but that's not true. I love him and he loves me. I don't want to wait anymore. It's going to be special and amazing. I know it.

Tasha closed her eyes and saw in her memory the night she and Josh lost their virginity together. Hannah had told her it would hurt the first time but it would get better. Tasha's palms had been clammy and she'd been afraid to let Josh hold her hand, but he'd understood, and even showed her how clammy his own hands had been. Josh was that kind of guy. He always went out of his way for the ones he loved.

Josh drove them to his family's vacation house in Wawona. The Halvorsens had already closed the cabin for the winter so there was little chance of anyone finding them. The bite in the air signaled fall was giving way to winter and it took her breath away, but the landscape was filled with western white pine, mountain hemlock and lodgepole pine, creating an oasis of natural beauty that made her feel safe and cherished. It was perfect.

The old house creaked with the wind, but Josh cranked up the radiator heater and grabbed plenty of blankets, some of which had been in his family for generations, and he warmed her from within with the love shining from his eyes.

Tasha blinked against the sudden burn in her eyes and swallowed the odd lump in her throat. She'd been right; that night was special and it had been perfect.

In all her life that moment stood out as the most pure in its innocence. They learned together the magic of two bodies coming together to create something close to knowing God. The fleeting pain faded under the gentle yet inexperienced hands of a boy she'd given her heart and soul to, and Tasha—even in her youth—knew not everyone was so lucky.

Tasha closed the notebook and hugged it to her chest as if somehow she could draw the emotion from the pages and experience that purity just once more. To remember that sex wasn't awful, that it didn't come with feelings of shame and humiliation, and that it was possible to laugh and play in the arms of a lover without wanting to run and hide from your own desire.

Something wet slid down her cheek and she realized tears were coursing from her eyes. Tasha groaned and wiped them away before hastily replacing the notebook and interlocking the tops of the box together.

Visiting the past was dangerous, not just for the bad memories that lurked—but for the good ones, too.

Sometimes, the good ones were worse.

CHAPTER ELEVEN

TASHA WATCHED AS NATALIE loaded their dad into her car for his weekly visit to the senior center and wondered if Natalie was right. She hated the tension between Nora and herself. It didn't feel natural, and the continuing hostility scraped at her raw nerves. She'd received an e-mail from her director asking when she was returning. Tasha didn't have an answer just yet, so her reply was vague. But she yearned to go back to what she'd known for so many years. There was comfort in routine and helping others. Yet…a strange, almost foreign part of her mind kept reminding her of times in Emmett's Mill that were wonderful and alive. It made her question if what she did now made her happy.

Josh was nearly done with the job. The frigid yet clear skies helped. If it had rained or snowed, it would've put a significant delay on the schedule. Christopher had come again with Josh to put up the new drywall and all that remained were the finishing touches.

Tasha secretly enjoyed having Josh in the house, and even though Christopher wasn't the most communicative, she wanted the chance to get to know him better but wasn't entirely sure how to ask or if she should even try. Josh was incredibly sensitive when it came to his son, not that she blamed him.

Josh's presence felt like a buffer between her and the grief that hovered like a vulture waiting for her to drop. The sounds of him working down the hall soothed the anxiety that was a constant presence. Yet, she wasn't sure if she had the same effect on Josh, and the knowledge was bothersome. Tasha could practically see the tension stiffening his shoulders and kinking the thick band of muscles in his neck and chest. She was shocked to realize the thought of easing his rigid muscles was not an unwelcome one. In fact, the mental picture of rubbing her palms along the solid length of his back warmed her insides in a pleasant way that should've made her wary but instead sent dark thrills down her spine. Tasha's cheeks flushed and she palmed one to feel the blood rushing.

The sound of plastic rustling jostled Tasha out of her thoughts, and Josh walked down the hallway toward the kitchen where she was standing. He wiped sweat from his forehead and Tasha wondered how his body worked up the moisture under such inhospitable working conditions.

"It's looking good," she offered as he helped himself to a glass of water from the dispenser on the refrigerator. "You can hardly tell how awful it looked before."

"I'm glad the weather is holding. Makes the work go faster." He finished the water and turned to leave, but a thought had come to Tasha in a flash and she was about to act on it before she lost her nerve.

"Josh…" she started, and he stopped expectantly. "I've been thinking of taking a trip up to Yosemite while I'm here…it's been a long time since I've been up there and I wondered if you and Christopher wouldn't mind going with me."

Tasha held her breath as a myriad of emotions ranged over his face and she sensed his conflict as if she were experiencing it herself. "Nothing romantic," she assured him softly, though at her words a twinge of disappointment followed. "I just don't want to go alone, and right now I'm not really on the best of terms with my sisters. I'm asking as a friend."

"Things bad?" he asked, surprising her with his interest.

"Nothing we can't get over—eventually, but right now…I don't think an hour car ride is advisable."

He chuckled, and the sound made her smile, too.

"I haven't been up to Yosemite in a while," Josh said, rubbing his chin, his expression thoughtful. "And getting Christopher to do something other than fiddle with those computers would be a plus. Sure," he slowly agreed, adding, "he's not really the outdoors type, but as much as I hate to admit Carrie might be right about something, I'm beginning to agree with her about how much time Chris spends on the computer. Getting out of the house might be good for us both."

"Carrie's concerned about his computer use?" Tasha asked carefully, knowing Josh was touchy about the subject.

He eyed her warily. "A little."

"Why? What's he doing?"

"Nothing bad, he just tends to spend a lot of time on it. Carrie wants him to be an athlete."

"Like you," she surmised.

"Yeah, I guess."

"She must think highly enough of you still to want her son to be like you."

Josh glowered. "That's not why she wants him to

be an athlete. It has everything to do with her ego, not Chris."

"She's his mother. I'm sure she just wants what's best for him," Tasha reproached him lightly, knowing by the tight press of his lips that he wasn't pleased, but she couldn't imagine a mother not wanting the best for her child. She never thought she'd see herself aligning her views with Carrie's, but she didn't see where Josh's anger came from.

"And I'm his father and I think she's making a big deal out of nothing."

Tasha nodded, letting the subject drop. Somehow she'd just severed the connection between them and the resulting space left her feeling out of sorts. "Josh, I'm sorry. I didn't mean to imply that you don't care. I know you do."

His face lost some of its tightness. "Thanks. I'm sorry, too. I guess I've been wearing my feelings on my shirtsleeve since the divorce. I didn't mean to snap at you."

"It's okay," she murmured. "Are we still on for Yosemite?"

He eyed her contemplatively, then nodded. "I'd like that."

"How about Saturday?" she suggested, noting

how quickly her mood lifted with his agreement. "The weather is supposed to be relatively mild, although up in the park it'll still be pretty cold. Probably low fifties. Make sure Chris bundles up."

Josh cracked a smile. "Always taking care of people, aren't you?"

Tasha grinned, though her cheeks warmed a little. "Can't help it, I guess. It's that eldest-sister thing I suppose."

Josh's expression softened, and for an instant Tasha saw the boy she'd once known; the boy who was always there for her, who allowed her to cry on his shoulder and held her sweater in the cafeteria line so she didn't have to balance it on her arm along with her lunch tray. His thoughtfulness was his hallmark. If anyone was always taking care of other people, it was Josh. His eyes cleared and Tasha felt Josh withdraw even though his subtle smile didn't fade. "Saturday it is. I'll pick you up at your hotel around eight?"

"Sounds good," Tasha murmured, ignoring the flicker of excitement in her stomach. "I appreciate you doing this," she added.

He smiled and shook his head in amusement. "Don't mention it. A day in Yosemite sounds great."

"I'm glad you feel that way. Sometimes I feel like I've leaned on you too much."

"You haven't," he assured her. "That's what friends are for, right?"

Are we friends? She wanted to ask but didn't. Tasha smiled and thanked him instead. She wanted his friendship. If things were different, she might be tempted to want more.

JOSH HOLLERED FOR Christopher one more time as he headed toward the truck with extra blankets. It was a wild idea, but he'd remembered that Tasha used to love to ice-skate at the Curry Village rink and thought they could swing by before lunch at the Ahwahnee Hotel. The Ahwahnee was an upscale place, but since everything in the park was expensive, he figured they ought to pay for something worth buying.

"Chris…sometime today, please," he shouted after another glance at his watch. What was that kid doing in there? "We're going to be late."

"Why can't I just stay here?" his son's voice whined from the bedroom. "I don't know how to ice skate and hiking in subzero weather isn't very appealing."

"Christopher Angelus Halvorsen, turn off that

computer and get your ass out here before I ground you from all access to that damn thing."

Christopher grumbled but appeared nonetheless. "When did you turn into a dictator?"

"When you turned into a hermit," Josh shot back without missing a beat. "There's more to life than whatever you've got going on in cyberspace."

"Doubtful."

Josh chose to overlook Chris's ill humor; he was actually looking forward to the day and he figured once Christopher was out of the house, he'd enjoy it, too.

Josh pulled up to the small hotel and saw Tasha waiting outside her door. She was appropriately bundled in a pink puffy jacket, jeans and warm Ugg boots. Her hands were shoved deep within her jacket pockets and her cheeks were pink from the cold, but a warm smile wreathed her beautiful mouth. Damn, if she didn't look like something out of a catalog. Josh shifted in his seat, catching the hungry look in his eyes from the rearview mirror. Great. That's all he needed Chris to see. He wasn't ready to answer questions, not even his own, much less his son's.

Still, his gaze lingered longer than he'd intended, as if drinking in her appearance, and Chris caught him. "We used to be more than friends," he found himself explaining until he realized he was only making himself look suspect. "Never mind. Hop in the back. Here she comes. And," he added, twisting to give his son a serious look, "best behavior, okay?"

Christopher rolled his eyes in annoyance. "What do I look like, twelve?"

Josh chuckled but didn't have time to retort for Tasha was almost to the door and he realized he was still just sitting there. Hopping from his seat, he ran around to the other side and opened the door for her.

"Josh, you didn't have to do that," Tasha said, but her soft gaze was clearly appreciative. "It's not like this is a date."

"I know," he said gruffly. "But there's nothing wrong with opening the door for a lady…even if she's just a friend."

"You're right." Tasha nodded and slid into the truck. "By all means, please exert your gentlemanly duties."

"Are you guys going to talk like that all day? If so, let me out at the next stop," Christopher groused from the backseat.

"Best behavior, Chris," Josh reminded him, and Chris sighed. "Thank you."

Tasha looked at him, concerned. "We don't have to go if this isn't a good time…"

He put the truck into gear and pulled onto the main street. "It's a perfect time. We're going to have a great day."

TASHA STARED AT THE overwhelming beauty of Yosemite National Park and wondered how she managed to stay away for so long. There was something spiritual about the park's natural beauty. She could almost feel good energy pouring into her, invigorating her senses and reminding her why it was great to be alive. She sent a wide smile to Josh and she knew he understood what she felt. Her breath plumed before her, the wintry climate nothing to scoff at, but she felt incredibly peaceful inside. "I'd forgotten how much I love this place," she admitted. "When I was a kid there wasn't a summer I didn't come up here to swim in the river or go hiking."

"Yeah, I know. I was with you half the time," Josh said.

"That's right." Tasha smiled. She tapped her head lightly. "There's a few good memories up here."

Josh cracked an embarrassed smile in return. "For me, too."

"This place is boring. It doesn't even have an

Internet café. How am I supposed to check my e-mail?" Christopher said, giving his father a dark look.

Josh clapped his hands together and pointed toward Curry Village. "No Internet today, buddy. Today…you're going to experience the bumps and bruises and sore behind of ice-skating."

Tasha gasped. "Is the rink still open?" she asked, barely able to contain her excitement. When Josh nodded, a grin in place, she did a little hop and gestured to Christopher. "You're going to love it! It's so much fun!"

Christopher didn't look so sure, but Tasha only laughed and hurried to the shack where the skate rentals were located. By the time Josh and Christopher pulled up the rear, she was already accepting a pair of black, completely worn skates. Josh gave the woman behind the counter his and Chris's sizes and soon they were sitting beside her on the cold bench.

Josh held up the old skate with a dubious expression. "These have seen better days," he noted, and Tasha laughed.

"Yeah, I think they're the same ones we used to wear when we were kids."

"Great…I'm going to kill myself," Chris said sourly, but one look from Josh and he was lacing them up.

Tasha stood carefully and wobbled the short distance to the rink. "Here goes nothing. I guess we'll see if this is something you don't forget."

Placing one foot on the frozen surface, she pushed off slowly and glided away, the rhythm coming to her easily. She made a few experimental turns to get her bearing and then skated over to where Josh and Chris were standing at the edge. Chris's expression had gone from dour to frightened. She reached out her hand.

"C'mon, I'll help you," Tasha offered to Chris. He seemed reluctant to accept her help until he flailed a little and almost fell on his behind. He quickly grasped her hand and Tasha sent a playful look Josh's way. "Looks like he inherited your feet," she said, gently leading Chris toward the wall. "Get your center of gravity first, then when you feel you can stand without wobbling, push off in a slightly diagonal direction with your dominant foot. Go slow, and if you get into trouble, here's the wall. But don't rely on the wall too much or else you'll never get the true hang of it," she said, letting Chris's hand go so that he could reach out to the wall.

Josh glided up to her and stopped with only the slightest wobble, and she rewarded him with a grin. "Not bad, but can you do this?"

Pushing off, she sailed across the ice into a semi-graceful turn that would've been incredibly impressive if she hadn't landed on her rear two seconds later.

Chris's and Josh's laughter blended with her own. "That didn't quite come off as I'd envisioned in my head," she admitted as she climbed to her feet.

"The Russian judge gives it a ten," Josh said with a mocking tone as he glided over to her, his expression mischievous. "I'd offer to kiss it but that might not be appropriate."

"Thank you for your restraint," Tasha said, returning his grin before motioning to Christopher to join her. He shook his head and looked suctioned to the wall. "C'mon, you can do it. Just give it a try. What's the worse that can happen? You fall on your butt. I already did that so it's your turn and then your dad's."

At that Josh gave her a look that said, "Thanks, I prefer to stay upright," but he followed as she skated over to Chris.

"One lap around the rink and you're off the hook," Josh offered, and Christopher's eyes lit up warily. "You can turn in your skates and sit by the fire pit until we're done. Fair enough?"

"'Fair' would've been giving me the option to stay home," Chris muttered.

"No, that would've been a democracy, and in this parental country, it's a dictatorship," Josh said with good humor despite his son's attitude. "What's it going to be?"

Christopher blew out a hard breath and then pushed off the wall with surprising agility for someone who'd only just put on skates ten minutes ago. Using careful glides, Christopher put some distance between himself and them.

"That's one determined kid you've got there," Tasha observed playfully, though a part of her saw much of Josh in the boy. When they'd been young, Josh had been the epitome of stubborn and headstrong. "He's definitely got that Halvorsen hard head going for him."

Josh sighed. "Yeah, recently, I've noticed that."

Tasha pushed off the wall and Josh followed. Soon they were skating side by side with matching strides.

"Having a hard time with him?" she asked.

He nodded. "Just recently. The divorce has been hard on him. Carrie… Well, she hasn't made seeing Christopher much of a priority lately, and when she does it's usually a disaster. She's always trying to get him to do things he doesn't enjoy."

"Like ice-skate?" Tasha teased, and he looked at her sharply until he realized she was kidding.

"Yeah." He gave a rueful grin. "Like ice-skating."

She twisted so that she was skating backward and Josh's face lit up.

"Impressive," he said as she turned back around. "Seems ice-skating is like riding a bike."

"Not exactly, I wouldn't try a jump right now," Tasha admitted with a laugh. "That's about the extent of my skating skills at this stage in my life. How about you?"

"Hey, I'm lucky I haven't landed on my ass. I think I'll stick to the easy stuff."

"Suit yourself," she answered cheekily, thoroughly enjoying herself and the company. Christopher made it to the other end of the rink and was gingerly making his way off the ice. She gestured toward Chris. "Didn't even fall once. Not bad. Seems he inherited your feet after all."

Tiny lines around his eyes crinkled as he chuckled, the sound deep and inviting, and Tasha wondered how any woman could walk away from this strong, solid man.

For a split second she found herself allowing shamefully catty thoughts about Carrie to surface, as if somehow it was all Carrie's fault she and Josh hadn't made it. But the moment she realized where her thoughts were going she stomped them down. It took two to make a marriage work…or cause it to fail. Sadness followed as she surreptitiously watched Josh, knowing somehow that he blamed himself for the breakup and it was eating him up inside. This hidden pain was what Sammy was talking about, what she'd sensed from the moment she saw him again.

Tasha wished she had the privilege to grasp his hand in her own, to show him with that one simple gesture that he wasn't alone and someone was there for him—but she couldn't do that. The invitation had not been extended and she knew better than to cross that boundary, but it felt natural to offer.

"Why do you blame yourself for the breakup of your marriage?" she asked.

He looked sharply at her as if surprised she'd ventured into such dangerous territory. She bit her lip but her words were already out there. "Someone's to blame, right? Might as well be me. I don't know how I ever got it into my head that I'd make a good husband."

Tasha couldn't help but wince at his statement. "I'm sure you were a wonderful husband," she countered with more conviction than she should've allowed. "I doubt you've changed so much from the man I used to know, and that man would've made a good partner."

She swallowed the lump in her throat and risked meeting his gaze. What she saw made her heart sink.

"I'm not that person anymore. Life has a way of changing you. I wasn't the best husband to Carrie and maybe she wasn't the best wife, but I know I could've tried harder."

"No one is perfect," she whispered, her heart breaking for him. "Stop beating yourself up over something that takes two."

He shook his head. "I don't need you to champion me, Tasha. It is what it is."

She bit back the urge to wail, What happened to the boy she used to know? He had to be in there somewhere. But, to what end? It wasn't as if she was going to be here when and if that person resurfaced. Sadness swamped her ability to respond. Not that it mattered, there wasn't much to say.

When she finally found her voice, she said, "You're right. It is what it is." Why the hell was she messing with fire? "I'm sorry I said anything."

"You all right?" he asked.

"I'm fine," she assured him. And she would be. Just as she always was…as soon as she left Emmett's Mill and Josh…behind.

CHAPTER TWELVE

JOSH AND CHRISTOPHER entered his parents' house and were immediately greeted by a hearty Halvorsen welcome. His brothers and nephew flanked his parents at the large oak table, his mother looking frightfully outnumbered by the various men in the room, and there was enough food covering every square inch to feed a squadron.

"You're late, Boo," his mother called out, using his childhood nickname and causing him to grimace. "Don't give me that look. Come, sit down. We almost didn't wait."

Josh bent down to kiss his mother's cheek before taking his place. "How you doing, Ma?"

"Can't complain. How's the Simmons job coming along?" she asked, reaching for the bowl of peas to hand to him. "I heard a tree went through the wall?"

His father scooped a large bite of mashed potatoes. "Heck of a thing, considering what Gerald's going through with Missy and all."

"Yeah, he's taking it pretty hard," Josh said, accepting the bowl and giving himself a healthy portion before handing it to Chris. "Natalie's running herself ragged trying to keep his head above water, and for some reason Tasha and Nora aren't getting along."

"That's a shame," clucked his mother, shooting a quick glance at Sammy. "You're real close with Nora, what's going on?"

Sammy grimaced. "Aww, Ma, why you asking me that? If I tell you what Nora's been filling my ear with, Josh is bound to throw his mashed potatoes at me and then it'll feel weird when I go to ask Tasha out."

Sammy acted as if he were poised to duck, but that damnable smirk wasn't far from his expression, telling everyone he was pulling Josh's leg. Because of that, Josh reined the impulse to growl and kept his expression purposefully neutral. Except, the thought of Sammy going out with Tasha rubbed him in a million different wrong ways and he was a terrible actor. "Stick to your brainless bimbos," Josh advised. "Tasha's way out of your league and definitely not your type."

"Josh," his mother admonished. "That's no way to talk about your brother's *friends*. I happen to think

Nora is a solid woman with a good head on her shoulders."

Sammy piped in. "Yeah!"

"I wasn't talking about Nora. She's too smart to throw her lot in with Sammy, which is probably why they've managed to stay friends for so long."

His father chuckled but otherwise remained silent on the issue of Sammy's predilection for less-than-brainy beauties. It was a running joke in the Halvorsen family; with their crew nothing was sacred, it seemed. Sammy valued two things in a woman, a sizable rack and the good sense not to press for a commitment. Even though his behavior was less than heroic, Sammy never failed to enjoy a steady stream of women running after him, just itching to be the next casual fling of Sammy Halvorsen. Frankly, Josh didn't get it. Maybe that was his problem. He invested too much of himself in others.

Dean looked to Christopher, who appeared more out of place among the Halvorsen men than a weed at Versailles, and gestured. "Brandon tells me you're some kind of computer genius. You managed to clear his hard drive of some nasty virus he picked up while trying to download from some crack site."

"Crack?" Mary Halvorsen repeated in alarm before

sending a concerned look toward her oldest grandson. "What are you doing at a crack site, for heaven's sake?"

"It's not what you think, Nana," Christopher interjected, grinning, though the tips of his ears reddened.

"Well, then, what is it?" she asked.

"It's a Web site that lists the registration codes for software. You download the crack and it allows you to use the software without paying for it."

Mary turned to Brandon, eyes afire. "Brandon Dean Halvorsen…are you telling me you're *stealing* from the Internet?"

"Nana, it's no big deal. Everyone does it," Chris said in Brandon's defense.

In truth, this was the first time Josh had ever heard of such a thing and it made him a little uneasy. "It is stealing, though," he said, and Dean agreed.

"I told Brandon no more of that stuff. The virus was bad enough, but what if he got busted for Internet fraud or something," Dean added. "Better not to mess with it."

"Dad—" Brandon started, but Josh's father decided to interject.

"We're an honest family," he said. "Stealing's stealing…no matter how you package it. I don't want to hear of any of my kin doing something so dirty. Hear me?"

Brandon looked chastised as he agreed, but Josh caught the subtle look of disdain on his own son's face. Clearly, he thought little of this Internet stealing and considered his family's reaction overbearing. Josh withheld a sigh, realizing he was going to have to have a serious sit-down talk with his son about morals, ethics and values.

CHRISTOPHER SAT OUTSIDE with Brandon while the rest of the adults talked about stuff that didn't interest either one of them and counted the moments until he could get back to his computer.

"Thanks for killing that virus," Brandon said, and Christopher nodded. "I thought my hard drive was toast. How'd you do it?"

Christopher scoffed at Brandon's impressed tone. "That's nothing. A kindergartner could've cleaned your drive."

Brandon bristled. "I'm no kindergartner and I couldn't get it out."

"No offense, Brandon, but you're not exactly a genius on the computer. You're still using Windows for an operating system."

"What do you use?"

Christopher gave him a bored look. "Currently...Linux, but I've used others."

Brandon frowned. "What are you…some kind of hacker?"

Christopher smiled, enjoying the power he felt at having superior knowledge on something. He wasn't good at sports but he could hack into anything he chose. "Yeah…something like that."

"What have you hacked into?" Brandon asked, his tone dubious. "Like banks and shit?"

"Banks are for people with a desire to do hard time. Besides, what am I going to do with money I can't spend, because the minute I do, the feds will zero in on my location and arrest my ass? No, I'm more low profile. I only hack for personal stuff. Gaming, mostly."

"Games?" Brandon looked at him dumbly. "What kind of games?"

"You ever played Zenith Rising?" Christopher asked.

"Yeah, once or twice. It was pretty cool. The new one's coming out in a few months, right?"

"I've already played it," Christopher said smugly.

"Bullshit. That's impossible."

Christopher laughed. "Nothing's impossible if you know what you're doing. Me and my friend OgDog have been playing it for weeks. We downloaded the testing version and we have it half solved. It's even better than the first one."

Brandon's expression faltered. "Dude...what if you get caught?"

Again, Christopher smirked. "I won't."

TASHA CAME FROM THE KITCHEN and stopped when she saw her father sitting in his recliner in the dark, the only light in the room coming from the low flames crackling in the fireplace.

She was tempted to turn around and leave him to his brooding, but she sensed his grief as if it were a palpable thing sitting in the room beside him, whispering sad words into his ear in a voice only he could hear.

And it didn't feel right to leave him like that.

Natalie and Nora had already gone home for the evening, which only left Tasha to check on him.

"Dad?" She walked into the room reluctantly, shamefully aware of how much she wanted to pretend she didn't see his pain. She'd learned years ago her father wasn't infallible, but seeing him sitting in his chair, shrunken and defeated, made that realization that much more crystal clear in her mind.

He didn't acknowledge her presence as she sat down on the sofa beside his recliner. "How you doing?"

Such dumb, inane questions. She tried again.

"What do you think of the bereavement group Natalie enrolled you in?"

At that he gave a soft snort. "Talking to some group isn't going to change the fact my Missy is gone," he said sourly. "The only reason I go is to get Natalie to relax. The girl is going to give herself an ulcer." He sent a short look at Tasha. "You should talk to her. Get her to settle down."

"She's worried about you," Tasha said quietly. "And you know she won't stop until she thinks you're okay."

Gerald's stricken expression told her he didn't think he'd ever see that day.

"Dad…I'm not going to tell you that some day the pain will fade, because I don't know if that's true." Her own hadn't. "But each day it's going to get easier to breathe, until one day you'll wake up and it won't feel as if an elephant is sitting on your chest."

She held his gaze until he chose to look away with an audible sigh that pulled at her heart. He turned his stare to the dying flames. "Sometimes…" He stopped, his voice cracking from pent-up emotion. He shook his head. "Forget it."

"What, Dad?" She wanted to know. "Please, tell me."

His lip quivered and she thought the light caught

tears shining in his eyes. "Sometimes, I swear, I hear her voice," he said, breaking down for a moment before pulling himself together in some semblance of control. "But I know it's not her. My Missy is gone."

Tasha didn't know what to say. A part of her wished she'd been the one to sense her mother's presence, just so she could grasp a hint of her essence, but it made sense that if her mother's spirit was indeed hanging around, that she would seek the man she'd spent the last forty years with. She sighed, seeking the right words. "Maybe she was trying to comfort you," Tasha offered, but her father scoffed at the idea.

"She's dead, Natasha," Gerald said. "She's not coming back." Heavy silence followed. Then Gerald struggled out of his recliner. Tasha watched as he walked stiffly from the room. He surprised her when he turned at the hallway. "I miss her, Tasha…more than I ever thought possible."

Tasha swallowed. "I know, Dad," she said solemnly. "We all do."

Gerald nodded curtly and left the room.

Tasha heard Natalie's voice in her head advising her to sit down with their father and talk things through, but it seemed simpler and less painful to just leave as she had before. Except, even as the coward in her heart whispered that half truth, another part of her shunned that idea. It wasn't simpler to walk away, not for her family. She couldn't possibly leave with everyone—most notably Natalie—holding on to their sanity by their fingertips.

She sighed and curled her legs underneath her. Although it was late, Tasha didn't feel like driving to her hotel. The house had settled with familiar creaks and groans, the warmth in the room lulling her with its comfortable embrace. Gazing at the embers, she drifted into a relaxed state, happy to just veg and let her mind rest.

Josh's face floated into view and she smiled softly. In the privacy of her mind, she enjoyed the memory of their trip to Yosemite. Being around him was as natural as breathing. The day had been near perfect until the end. Her smile faded slowly. It was unhealthy to wallow in the past, yet one could say that's all she's been doing since she left Emmett's Mill. Still, in this instance, she couldn't help but recall how safe and secure she'd felt around Josh—reminding her of times so far gone it ought to feel like a faded memory rather than the brightest spot in her life.

Tasha shut her eyes against the sadness creeping up on her. It seemed her life was a series of sad moments. Was that ever going to change? Or was that the card she'd been dealt in this lifetime?

She hoped not—she wanted so much more.

Another sigh escaped and she buried her face in her arm, hating the maudlin turn of her own thoughts, hating the trapped feeling that never seemed far, no matter how long she ran.

She craved someone she could cling to when the memories crowded her space, invading every facet of her life. A man whose arms would provide a safe haven from the pain lodged in her heart and soul.

Except, she knew there was only one person who fit the bill…and he was the person fate had taken from her and given to someone else.

CHAPTER THIRTEEN

JOSH FIDGETED WITH THE phone, vacillating between asking Tasha to dinner or not. Christopher was spending the night at Brandon's and he had the whole house to himself. Unfortunately, the longer he sat there listening to the silence, the more he was convinced it didn't really appeal to him. A consequence of growing up in a household full of boys, he supposed.

It was one of the many differences between him and Carrie; she'd grown up an only child and preferred the quiet, while Josh felt most at home when there were ten different things going on at once.

He stared at the numbers, hating the place he was caught in. Didn't seem a place a grown man was supposed to be. Josh realized with a start that he was a bundle of nerves. He released an embarrassed chuckle and resolutely hung up the phone. He wasn't a kid and he certainly didn't need to start acting like one.

Striding from the room, intent on finding a project to occupy his mind, he was halfway to the garage when he did an about-face.

One dinner didn't mean anything. People sat down to eat all the time, didn't mean they were sharing something special.

Just food and companionship.

Yep.

He dialed Tasha's number and ignored the warning bells that clanged as anticipation overruled everything else.

And the pope wears Betty Boop underwear.

TASHA SMOOTHED THE nonexistent wrinkles from her dress and waited nervously for Josh to arrive. She still couldn't believe he'd asked her to dinner. It had been on the tip of her tongue to decline, but when she realized she really wanted to go, she'd agreed.

Tasha was careful not to read anything into it. Neither was ready for any kind of relationship. The very thought was ridiculous, and she fiercely reminded herself of that simple logic when a traitorous flutter erupted in her stomach.

A knock sounded at the door and she hurried to answer. Josh stood in the bright hotel light and she nearly sucked in her tongue at his appearance. His tailored brushed suede coat, coupled with faded blue jeans and a snow-white linen shirt, was perfectly set off by the worn cowboy boots, giving him a roguish air that sent her pulse racing. His gaze seemed to travel from her toes to the top of her head, as if imprinting her image with every synapse in his brain, and Tasha gave him a cautious smile.

"You look beautiful," he said in a husky murmur. "Every man in Emmett's Mill is going to be jealous tonight."

"Don't be silly. It's just me and I'm no one special."

The look in his eyes stole her breath. It said everything she felt in her heart but didn't have the right to voice.

"Shall we?" He offered his arm and she took it.

All manner of inappropriate thoughts raced through her mind as he led her through the lobby to his awaiting truck, struck by the incredible sensation that this felt like a date when it shouldn't.

Enjoy the moment, for crying out loud! Nora's voice rang in her ears and she actually winced. *Fine. I will.*

Josh pulled into the Grill and she turned to him in surprise. "Are you sure? Chances are high we'll run into someone we know."

He grinned at the anxiousness in her tone. "Tasha, you're the best company I've had in months. I don't care who sees us having dinner together. Unless, of course, you prefer somewhere else," he added.

She smiled against the trepidation she felt in her chest and shook her head.

"All right, then, bring your appetite, because I hear the burgers here are nothing short of amazing. Of course, this all comes from Sammy, and you might have to take his word with a grain of salt. I wouldn't say his tastes are all that discerning when it comes to food. As long as it's hot and reasonably salted, he's good to go."

Tasha laughed and they entered the bustling restaurant. Immediately, a voice rang out and Tasha instinctively drew closer to Josh until she recognized the person who was waving them over to their table.

"Josh Halvorsen, you lucky son of a bitch, how are you?"

Karl Masterson, a graduate the same year as Josh and Tasha, looked nothing like he did in high school. Round and portly with ruddy, wind-chapped cheeks, he rose where he sat with his family and pumped Josh's hand enthusiastically. "I heard you'd moved back to town but figured since I hadn't seen you yet, those brothers of yours must be keeping you pretty busy."

Josh nodded. "Busy is good. Keeps the mind from thinking too much."

"I hear ya there." Karl boomed with laughter until his eyes fell on Tasha, who had done her best to draw little attention to herself. "Natasha Simmons," he said, ending in a low whistle, which immediately made her uncomfortable. Karl didn't threaten her; she just didn't enjoy that much male attention.

"How are you doing, Karl?" she asked politely.

"Can't complain. This here's my wife, Angela, and our two daughters, Matty and Dylan." Tasha inclined her head toward Karl's wife but discreetly tugged at Josh's coat.

"Good to see you, Karl," Josh said with a warm grin. "But we're starving and need to get a table."

The hostess sat them a few moments later. As Tasha took her seat in a cozy booth away from a large party, which by the sounds of their hooting and hollering was the evening's first pit stop before the real fun in the lounge began, she released the breath she'd been unconsciously holding.

"You okay?" Josh asked, concerned.

"Fine." She gave him a bright smile but averted

her eyes, as if searching for their waitress. "But I am hungry. I think I could probably eat a whole cow."

Josh chuckled, but the sound held some reservation. He sensed something was wrong, she knew it, but she wasn't about to tell him the real reason she was suddenly on edge. Besides, tonight was about enjoying each other's company. She sent him another smile, this time with more enthusiasm, and he relaxed.

"Thanks for coming out with me tonight," Josh said. "I really didn't want to sit around the house with nothing but my own thoughts to keep me company."

She understood that. "We all gotta eat, right?"

He nodded. "We do. And if someone else is doing the cooking, I'm all for it."

"Still not much of a gourmet, huh?" she asked, teasing.

He shook his head ruefully. "No, and Chris and I have the sour stomachs to prove it. Since Carrie... Well, we've been roughing it."

"Carrie was a good cook?"

"Yeah, pretty good. Nothing fancy, but then my tastes never ran toward that stuff. Just good old-fashioned meat and potatoes."

Tasha smiled. She used to tease Josh for his

stubborn refusal to try Thai food once when they were out for dinner. She'd tried every manner of cajoling to get him to just give it a taste but he wouldn't budge. It was nice to see some things hadn't changed.

After they'd placed their order, Tasha took a look around the crowded restaurant for more familiar faces. She couldn't stop her muscles from tensing even as she made an effort to appear nonchalant. It was slim, but she had a fear of running into Diane Lewis again. Flinching at the thought, she caught Josh's perplexed stare.

"What's wrong?" he asked, his intent gaze drying up the glib statement she was about to offer. "If you'd like to go someplace else, I don't mind."

"Josh…the restaurant is fine. There's just a few people I'd rather not run into," she said, dropping her stare to the neatly folded napkin in her lap. She risked a small laugh. "And usually when I visit, I avoid town."

"May I ask who you are trying to avoid?"

"No." She laughed, the sound sad and desperate to her own ears. Then she waved away his concern. "Don't worry about it. It's fine. Really."

"It's not," he disagreed. "But if you don't want to tell me, I'm not going to pressure you. Just know that if you ever need a shoulder…mine is always available. That's what friends are for, right?"

She swallowed the lump in her throat at his offer. "Thank you, Josh."

"Don't mention it."

Josh let the topic go, steering the conversation to neutral areas, and Tasha slowly relaxed. She listened as he talked about Christopher—his love for his son was evident in his tone and sent warm tendrils of some unnamed emotion curling through her body—and she chatted about her work in developing countries.

"Coming back here, it almost seemed like déjà vu," she admitted, looking up quickly to gauge his reaction. When he smiled, she added in a husky murmur, "I have a lot of memories of me and you in a darkened vehicle. Good memories," she added.

He broke into a wide grin. "Remember that time your dad caught us making out in my old Dodge Charger? God, I thought he was going to shoot me right then and there."

Tasha giggled and it felt good. "We thought we were being so smart by parking down the driveway with the headlights off. Who knew my dad was waiting and saw us drive up from his bedroom window. I was grounded for two weeks."

"I remember," he said, groaning. "I thought it was the longest two weeks of my life."

"You and me both."

An easy silence passed between them, and as the laughter eased from their mouths Tasha's thoughts turned unexpectantly. "What went wrong with us?" she asked, realizing too late what she'd just done. Embarrassed, she said, "Scratch that. I'm sorry. I have no idea where that came from."

Josh's attitude turned solemn, but he surprised her with an answer. "Immaturity."

Good, safe answer. She agreed. "You're right. We were just two young, dumb kids. I suppose high-school romances aren't meant to last for that very reason. We were crazy to try a long-distance relationship."

"Yeah, I guess so."

Since they'd already broached the subject, Tasha asked another question that had always plagued her.

"Why Carrie? I mean, how did you two hook up?"

Josh grimaced, and Tasha sensed there was something to the story that he didn't enjoy telling. He exhaled loudly and said, "More dumb-kid stuff. I guess you could say there was a time period when I was a little lost. I was partying a lot and happened to see

Carrie one night at a big New Year's Eve bash in Stockton. We hit it off. She liked to party, I liked to party, so it seemed good. Then she turned up pregnant."

Tasha understood immediately. Josh's moral compass would only steer him in one direction if faced with that situation. It was one of his most endearing qualities.

"But I don't regret it. Chris is a great kid. A father couldn't ask for a better boy."

Warmth suffused her body as she gently grasped his hand. "A boy couldn't ask for a better father."

He looked at her and she had to turn away, before he saw the sudden tears that pricked her eyes. She hadn't meant to, but she couldn't help but mourn the future that she'd been denied.

She'd envisioned a future with Josh, had foolishly assumed in her childish naiveté that even though they'd broken up, when the time was right, fate would put them in each other's path again.

"She was a lucky woman," she finally said with a bright smile that felt worn around the edges but hopefully didn't show how ragged she felt inside.

His mouth tightened, but he only shrugged in response. "My son is all that matters at this point," he said.

She nodded, her throat closing at the emotion squeezing her heart. "I understand completely. That's how it should be."

Things had been going so well, she'd almost forgotten why they couldn't pick up where they left off just as she'd imagined. Their instant, undeniable chemistry almost supported that childish hope, but Tasha knew there were no fairy-tale endings for her. Her place was not in Emmett's Mill. She couldn't hide the fear that caused beads of sweat to pop along her forehead anytime she drove past Crystal Aire Drive, and Josh was dealing with the aftereffects of a broken marriage. But sitting there with Josh within touching distance, his very scent soothing her nerves, was insidiously cruel as it taunted her with a possibility that was simply an illusion.

"Hey," he admonished lightly, making a direct attempt to change the mood. "Enough of this serious talk, okay? We're two friends enjoying dinner. From this point forward, the topics of divorce, disillusionment and heartbreak aren't allowed. Sound good?"

She smiled through the tears threatening to embarrass her. "Sounds perfect. Let's find that waitress.

I feel like I haven't eaten in a week," she declared, immensely grateful for his ability to lift her mood.

"That's the Tasha I remember—the woman with the appetite of a horse and not afraid to show it."

She grinned and he motioned for their server.

DINNER LONG FINISHED, it was several hours before they left the restaurant, both so busy catching up that they lost track of time.

Josh held the door open for her as they left, and as Tasha stepped over the threshold, the sound of a drunken female screech filled the small square, drawing her gaze to a thin blond woman stumbling off the curb and nearly into the street as a man tried catching her unsuccessfully.

"It's my goddamn birthday!" the woman shouted as the door of Gilly's swung shut. "That's no way to treat a paying customer!"

"C'mon baby, let's take this party to my place," suggested the man, but the woman pushed past him to give the door a resounding bang with her fist, then howled at the pain. The man came up behind her and slid his hands up her chest and blatantly fondled her breasts through the tight sweater she was wearing until she slapped his hands.

"Get off me," she said, but he wasn't deterred and tried planting his mouth on hers until she pushed him. "Get away. Don't touch me."

The door opened and a burly man blocked the entrance even as she tried shoving past him. "You're cut off, Chloe. Go home."

Tasha gasped as she peered a little harder, barely recognizing the disheveled woman as the girl she'd babysat years ago. Pain lanced her heart as the woman wobbled and tried to move past the man again and ended up on her ass this time. The man who'd been hoping to get lucky wandered off, leaving her in the muck of the gutter.

"Do you know her?" Josh asked, puzzled.

"I used to," she answered, tugging at Josh's hand. "We have to help her." She urged him to follow as she crossed the street and went to the woman who had begun to cry softly.

Josh glared at the bouncer, but the man only shrugged, saying, "She's your problem now," and disappeared inside the bar, music blaring.

Tasha tried getting Chloe's attention but it took several moments before the woman could focus. She smelled like a distillery and looked ten years older than her actual age. "Chloe, honey, it's Tasha.

C'mon, we'll take you home," she said, helping Chloe to her feet.

"Tasha?" Chloe slurred, recognition coming slowly. "Tasha Simmons? What are you doing here?"

"Helping you. C'mon, you have to stand up. I can't carry you."

"It's my birthday," Chloe said in a pained whisper, leaning heavily on Tasha and Josh. Her bleary gaze tormented, she said, "I hate my birthday."

"Once you reach a certain age no one likes their birthday, honey. Upsy daisy, let's go."

Chloe's knees went out on her, and if it weren't for Josh's quick reflexes, they both would've tumbled to the ground. Instead, Josh caught Chloe and hoisted her in his arms. Tasha sent him a grateful look and they walked to Josh's truck.

A soft snore against Josh's shoulder told them Chloe had passed out, and Tasha smoothed a lock of sweaty hair from Chloe's brow.

"I used to babysit her when she was a kid," Tasha murmured, wondering how Chloe Lewis had fallen so far from grace as to become a public spectacle. A horrid thought came to mind, but she shrugged it away. Bronson had been a monster but surely not a devil.

Josh slid Chloe into the front seat and Tasha climbed in beside her, locking the seat belt in place. "I guess we'll take her to her mom's place. That's the only thing I can suggest. She lives just outside of town in Whispering Oaks. Do you mind?"

"Not at all," he said, turning the ignition and slowly pulling out of the parking lot. "She's lucky you were there. No telling what kind of night she'd have ended with."

Tasha shuddered. She had a good idea.

"Has she always been a bit of a wild child?" he asked in a whisper.

Tasha shook her head. "Not the Chloe I remember. She was a good kid. Straight A's, honor roll, she was gearing for an Ivy league. I don't know what happened."

"Maybe she cracked under the pressure."

"Maybe," Tasha said, but the ugly thought had germinated inside her head. "Let's just get her home. I'll feel better when I know she's safe for the night."

They drove in silence to the Lewis house, and Tasha's gut muscles constricted as the familiar columns came into view. The automatic flood lamps came on, bathing the driveway in light, and in the backyard the sound of dogs barking brought a robed figure to the front door.

Josh and Tasha helped Chloe out of the truck and Tasha could tell by Diane's stricken expression she was in for a shock.

"Diane, we found Chloe outside Gilly's and decided to give her a ride home."

"Chloe? I didn't even know she was in town," Diane said as she came forward, shock registering on her lined face. Without the protective layer of expensive cosmetics, Diane's age was evident. "Yes, please bring her in."

They deposited Chloe on the nearest sofa and Tasha wanted nothing more than to make a quick getaway, but something was nagging at her and her mouth took control. "She doesn't live here anymore? In Emmett's Mill?"

"Chloe moved away when she turned eighteen. Last I heard she was living in Fresno. She moves around a lot, though. I haven't a clue where she's living now." Her gaze strayed to her daughter and a subtle spasm of pain rippled across her expression before she could hide it. "Thank you," she added, her posture stiffening ever so slightly. "I'll take it from here."

Tasha nodded and led the way back to the truck,

eager to get away from Diane, Chloe and the evidence that was staring her right in the face.

"You okay?" Josh asked as they climbed inside.

"Let's just get out of here," she said, tears choking her voice.

If her suspicion was correct—she hadn't been Bronson's only victim. And the realization soured the food in her stomach until she felt she was going to retch. It was bad enough how she'd suffered, but to think he might've done the unthinkable to his own daughter made her gag.

EVEN IN THE DARK JOSH COULD tell Tasha was on edge.

"Tasha, what's wrong?" he asked as he pulled into a parking space at her hotel. "Is it Chloe?"

He caught the shake of her head. "She was a great kid," she managed to say. "I can't believe how much she's changed."

"You never know how people are going to turn out," he said, gently agreeing.

She turned to him sharply, her eyes blazing. "No, some people don't change because they want to—it's forced on them. A person doesn't start out a stellar student and end up a drunk unless something happened to put them there."

"We don't know what happened in Chloe's life. Some people aren't as strong as others and life can beat a person down if they're not prepared."

Her breath came quickly as if she were struggling with something, and Josh ran his knuckle gently down the side of her jaw. She closed her eyes at the brief contact, and when she opened them again, there was a wealth of agony that cut him to ribbons for his ignorance. "Tasha…tell me what's bothering you. Please," he pleaded softly, but she only gave a short jerk of her head.

"I can't."

And then she bolted from the truck before he could stop her and practically ran to her room, leaving him to stare and wonder if Chloe wasn't the only one life had thrown a curve ball at.

CHAPTER FOURTEEN

JOSH KNEW HE'D PROMISED not to pressure her, but there was a gnawing sense of intuition that he couldn't ignore. Tasha was hiding something.

The next morning he knocked on her hotel-room door only to find she'd already left for her parents' house.

He drove to the Simmons place and found her outside, staring at the trees. She turned and saw him coming toward her. "Josh? What are you doing here so early?" she asked in surprise. "Is everything okay? Christopher?"

"Christopher is fine. I came to talk to you about last night."

She sighed heavily. "Josh, let it go."

"Not going to happen." He fell in step with her as she walked the property. "We're going to get to the bottom of this," he promised, and read fear in her eyes. "You can trust me."

She stammered a denial. "N-nothing's wrong, Josh. Please, stop asking."

He shook his head. "I've sensed it since I first saw you and I chalked it up to grief, but I think it goes deeper than grief and that's what worries me. When we first entered the restaurant your entire body tensed, and when we were talking to Karl…" He stopped, an awful thought coming to him. "Did Karl do something to you?"

"No, Karl didn't hurt me. I'm fine," she insisted, but there was an underlying panic in her tone. His heart rate began to thunder as his gut told him something terrible had happened to Tasha but she was trying to bury it. She blinked away the moisture he saw creeping into her eyes. "It's nothing you can fix. No one can."

"Let me try," he said gently, but she fisted her hands at her side. He cupped her hands in his own, coaxing the tension from her palms. "Whatever it is, I'll do my best to make you feel better," he promised, but fear was starting to curl in his belly. What had happened, for God's sake? He could think of only one thing that could crush a woman's spirit so completely and the thought was making him shake with trepidation.

"I…I…don't want to talk about it," she said, her voice tight with unshed tears, her cheeks deathly pale. "I can't."

"You can," he encouraged her softly. "I know you can. You're the strongest woman I know. There's nothing you can't do."

She shook her head in a wild, jerky motion. "I'm not strong. I couldn't fight him," she said, gulping for air. "I couldn't fight him. He…he was too big, too strong."

"What happened?"

Her expression stark, she whispered, "What do you think? I was raped."

Josh staggered under the suffocating weight of her revelation and struggled to comprehend the magnitude.

Oh, God, he wanted to moan. His mind balked at the possibility, bitter rage filling his mouth at the very idea. He'd kill the bastard with his bare hands. How could someone do that? Suddenly, Tasha's behavior made sense.

She'd been outgoing to the point of overly social in high school. Pretty, she'd always turned heads. Now he noticed she downplayed her natural good looks, not that it worked. She had a bone-deep grace that not even a pound of mud could cover. Son of a bitch, he swore.

He swallowed against the pain he read in her eyes. Beyond anything else he wished he could pull her into his arms and take away the memory. Short of that, he wanted her to know she didn't have to carry this burden alone.

"Tasha, whoever did this is the scum of the earth and deserves to die, but short of that, he's got one hell of an ass-kicking coming." She turned away, her reaction baffling him. It almost seemed she was protecting the bastard. "Tasha…tell me who did this."

"No."

"Why not?" he demanded, his hands already curling into fists, hungering for violence.

When she met his gaze again, the look in them was devoid of emotion.

"Because he's already dead."

TEARS STREAMED DOWN her face unchecked but she was frozen, unable to wipe them away or make them stop. Fear paralyzed her as Josh's gentle face contorted with rage and she could feel his body trembling.

His growl of frustration ended with a deep rumble, and she knew he was swallowing the carnage he wanted to wreak on her behalf.

Tasha felt nothing. It was as if she were watching

the scene from outside her body. Her revelation had stunned Josh and taken the fury out of his resolve, leaving in its place bewildered shock.

She sighed. "He died five years ago. Heart attack."

"Heart attack?" he repeated, quickly digesting the information. "He was an older man?"

Tasha felt herself nod. "My dad's age."

Revulsion crossed his strong features and she slammed back into her body, curling into herself. "So, you see, God has already taken care of things. There's no need for misplaced heroics," she said.

Josh cursed. "Were there ever charges filed?"

At that Tasha smothered a hysterical laugh. File charges against one of the best defense attorneys in town? If the case hadn't been laughed out of court, he would've painted her to look like some opportunistic slut out to destroy a good man, her family would've been ruined. She couldn't take the chance. She shook her head.

"Why not?" he asked, earning a derisive look that he didn't understand but she wasn't up to explaining. "Tasha, why would you let someone get away with that? What if there were other victims?"

Tasha thought of Chloe and swallowed a lump of guilt. "It was just easier to leave."

"Easier for who?" Josh demanded.

"Everyone."

He advanced toward her, but when she stiffened, he stopped, pain at her reaction in his eyes. "Tasha, let me help you. I can't stand to see you hurting like this."

"What's done is done, Josh. Nothing can change the past. Believe me, if there was a way, I'd have found it."

"I'll help you find a good therapist so you can work through this."

"And then what?" she asked. "It's not part of my future to ride off into the sunset with my handsome prince. I've come to realize this and I've stopped fighting it. I was dealt a different hand and I'm managing the best way I know how."

"You may have stopped fighting, but when you did you stopped living. Don't let this destroy you."

Too late. "You should go. I think we've said everything that can be said."

He held her stare. "No, we haven't. Not by a long shot," he promised, and advanced toward her, grabbing her gently by the shoulders so she could read the truth in his eyes. "You deserve justice. There must be something we can do."

"Like what? Dig him up and scream at his bones?

Drive to his wife's house and tell her what a monster she was married to? And then what? It won't change the facts. He did what he did and now he's dead. End of story. He didn't give a rip about my pain and I don't care to expose to the world what happened to me when I was too stupid to notice the warning signs!"

That last bit came from a dark and bitter place that she rarely allowed to see the light of day, but it flew out of her mouth like verbal vomit and she couldn't stop it. Tears sprang to her eyes and she tried to jerk out of his grasp, but he pulled her into his arms instead and she sagged against him.

"You aren't to blame," he said sternly, yet his touch was gentle as he caressed the back of her head. "He was a sick bastard who took advantage of a young woman who'd never been exposed to anyone so depraved. How could you have known what to watch for?"

She didn't answer but clung to Josh so tightly that if it were possible, they might've merged into one body. She'd seen Bronson's hungry looks when he thought she wasn't watching. But when her gut instinct told her to quit, the logical side of her brain had convinced her she was being ridiculous. It was Bronson—a man she'd known for years. He'd never do something so awful. A sob racked her body and Josh held her tighter. "I should've quit. I should've paid better attention. I should've… screamed."

"You worked for him?" Josh asked, astounded.

Tasha looked away. "Yes," she whispered.

"What a rotten bastard," he whispered into her hair. "Please let me help you get through this."

His plea filtered down through her tears. Good, sweet Josh. Always her champion. Tasha held on to him for one second longer, soaking up as much comfort from his embrace as possible, before resolutely pulling away. "Josh, you can't fix this," she said sadly. "And I won't drag you down with me. Just let it go. Please."

Josh started to protest, but something in her eyes snapped his mouth shut. After a long moment, he shook his head and turned on his heel.

As she listened to the sound of his truck pulling away, she stared at the tree line, hating her life.

She'd never wanted Josh to know what happened to her. His ignorance preserved a piece of her that was pure and innocent. Now that he knew, she felt dirty and exposed…and worse, heartbroken for the loss of the last part of her that was untouched.

GERALD EASED AWAY FROM the windowsill, unseen by either Tasha or Josh. Regret. Deep and heavy regret left a metallic taste in his mouth. An old painful conversation floated from his memory and he shook his head as if the motion would dislodge it. But the memory persisted.

"Dad…" Tasha had implored, her entire body shaking. "Please believe me. I wouldn't lie," she'd whispered.

The sound echoed in his skull and he winced. His own shameful answer returned to haunt him.

"Bronson Lewis is a good man! How could you say such a thing? My own daughter? For God's sake, Natasha! Bronson thinks of you as his own! What you're saying is impossible!"

Tasha's sobs rang in his ears, but her stricken expression was something he saw every night in his dreams. He'd forced his own daughter away because he couldn't believe his best friend would do something so repugnant. He remembered Missy's pale face, her blue eyes wide with fear, looking to him for guidance yet begging him to protect their daughter if she'd been hurt, and he'd failed them both.

Missy, bless her sweet soul, never said a cross word to him about the situation, trusting him to make the right decision, but he was too proud to admit he'd made the wrong choice. Horribly wrong. His friendship with Bronson ended abruptly, though Missy had tried to keep things friendly with Diane. He couldn't look at the man. Tasha's tear-streaked face stared back at him whenever he thought of rekindling anything.

His lips trembled. *Missy, I let you down.*

Worse, he betrayed Tasha. His firstborn.

A wave of remorse almost buckled his knees, but he straightened with a newborn sense of resolve. He could do his part to help his daughter. He owed her that much.

Just as his hand grasped the side-door handle, intent on righting a grievous wrong, a sudden crushing pressure in his chest took his breath away, causing him to stumble. He opened his mouth to call out, but it felt as if a giant hand had punched through his chest, squeezing his heart muscle to pulp. "Tash—" he gasped, black dots dancing before his eyes.

Collapsing, he barely felt his body connect with the hardwood floor. The black dots nearly converged until a radiant, white light split the darkness and he blinked slowly against its brilliance.

"My darling."

Missy's voice floated from the center of the blazing light and the pain subsided in his chest. "Missy?" he called out, struggling to sit up until a soft hand on his shoulder gently stilled his movement.

Missy, young and vibrant, achingly beautiful, knelt by his side and he started to babble like a baby until she shushed him.

"It's not your time. Our daughters need you."

"Missy…" Gerald cried, tears overflowing his eyes in the way he didn't allow at the funeral. "Missy, please. Don't leave me again."

It was a desperate plea, but he wasn't ashamed. He missed his wife in a way that was palpable.

She smiled and the light seemed to blaze brighter. "I'm always with you. In your heart…"

Missy's image began to fade and Gerald reached for her. She shook her head. "Be strong, Gerald. This is going…to hurt."

Her last words ended just as the light winked out and Gerald became painfully aware as volts of electricity kick-started his heart. Paramedics surrounded him and an oxygen mask was over his mouth and nose. Out of the corner of his eye he saw Tasha crying as she watched fearfully. He groaned as the paramedics hoisted the gurney to its full height and moved quickly from the house to the ambulance.

He tried to talk but his mouth felt numb. Extreme fatigue pulled at his eyelids and he gave in—his last thought was of his wife's smiling face.

CHAPTER FIFTEEN

TASHA WAS IN THE WAITING room when her sisters burst through the E.R. entrance, both wild-eyed with concern as they rushed to her side. Nora was the first to speak.

"What happened?"

"I don't know. I was outside and…I came in and found him by the side door. He was unconscious and his skin was gray. I called 9-1-1 and when the paramedics came they used the defibrillator on him."

"How long was he out?" Natalie asked.

Tasha shook her head. "I don't know. But he didn't look very good. They managed to get a pulse, but I don't think he regained consciousness."

"Are you okay?" Natalie asked, peering at Tasha.

Tasha nodded, but Nora caught the subtle shaking of her hands. She stepped forward and surprised Tasha by drawing her into a fierce hug. "He's going to be okay. No one is more stubborn than our dad," she whispered into Tasha's ear. "He's going to whip this and go back to his ornery self. You'll see."

Tasha held her sister for what seemed the longest moment until a doctor appeared in the doorway.

"Are you the family of Gerald Simmons?"

Tasha and Nora broke their embrace and all three sisters nodded.

"Your father has suffered a massive heart attack. Has he been under a lot of stress?"

"His wife, our mother, just died a few weeks ago," Natalie answered for them. "He took it pretty hard."

The doctor nodded. "He's going to need surgery to repair the damage. We'll let you know how it goes as soon as we're finished."

Natalie nodded and sank into a chair. Tasha and Nora followed. This time it was Tasha who provided comfort. "Nora's right. He's going to come through this with flying colors. I truly believe that."

"Tasha," Natalie said, her voice clogged with tears. "He's not invincible. I knew he wasn't taking good enough care of himself. I told him to stop eating those cookies but he refused to listen! Goddamn it!"

Natalie's rare show of anger was like a splash of cold water on Tasha's face. She'd sensed her sister was taking on too much, and seeing her teeter on the edge of a breakdown brought out Tasha's protective instincts.

"Stop that," she said, surprising both Nora and Natalie. "Don't take this on. Dad's health is his own business. None of us can be expected to hover over him like a mother hen."

"Easy for you to say, you've never stuck around," Natalie said.

Tasha drew back but forced herself not to take offense. "Nat, you're exhausted. Why don't you call Evan to come and get you—" Natalie started to protest. "It will be hours before we hear anything. I'll call as soon as the doctor gives us any news."

Nora piped in. "Tasha is right. Nat, you look like shit. You're no good to us if you collapse, too."

Natalie appeared wounded but nodded. "Fine. You promise to call the minute you hear anything?"

"Absolutely," Tasha promised.

"All right." Natalie rubbed her bloodshot eyes and went to call her husband.

Nora leaned back in her chair and Tasha grimaced at the soft pop that followed.

"Oh, I needed that," Nora groaned. "Who needs a chiropractor when you've got a stiff-backed chair handy."

"I'm not a chiropractor but I can tell that's really bad for your back," she said. "It's a bad habit to start, too."

"You can come out of big-sister mode," Nora said dryly, and Tasha acknowledged her with a tired grin. God, she had sounded like a nagging older sister. Then Nora nudged her playfully with her shoulder, saying, "When I get old I'll marry a chiropractor just so I can have someone around to put me back together."

"Like someone would marry you," Tasha returned with a snort.

Nora looked at her sharply until she realized Tasha was kidding. A wide, appreciative grin tilted the corners of her mouth. "Nice to see I'm not the only smart-ass in the family. I was beginning to think I was adopted."

Tasha grinned. "You were."

Despite the circumstances, Tasha allowed herself to relax a little. She hoped her father was in good hands. Hope was all she could do. Sighing, she turned to Nora.

"Are you happy?"

Nora did a double take. "What kind of question is that?"

Tasha shrugged. "A difficult one?"

"Of course it's difficult. Who's really happy nowadays?"

"So you're not?"

Nora exhaled loudly with annoyance. "Jeez, sis, could you have picked a more inappropriate moment to go all 'meaning of life' on me?"

Tasha chuckled. Nora was right. "Sorry. I just wondered."

"Well, stop wondering. I'm as freaking happy as the next girl out there who's single, self-employed and the biggest pain in the ass to her father."

"Pain in the ass, eh?"

"Yeah."

Tasha smiled. "Good. Someone's gotta to keep him on his toes."

An easy silence passed between them and Tasha realized she didn't know her baby sister, but she suspected the woman wasn't half bad.

"You and Dad were close," Nora remarked.

The statement rocked Tasha out of her cocoon of private thoughts. She weighed her answer. Giving too much information would only lead to more questions, and frankly, she thought they'd all had enough excitement for the day.

"Sure," Tasha said carefully. "As close as he is with all his daughters."

Nora's silence was telling. Tasha inhaled and offered a little more. "Well, you're right. Once we were close, but not as close as Mom and me. Mom was special."

Unexpected tears pricked her eyes and Tasha rubbed them out with her palm. When she looked at Nora again, the dull light reflecting from Nora's gray eyes saddened her.

"I was always mad at Mom for being so…weak," Nora admitted quietly. She looked to Tasha, waiting for recrimination, but when she sensed none she continued. "And Dad…he's such a hard-ass that it seems I'm always pissed off at him."

"He is a hard-ass," Tasha agreed, then swallowed the unpleasant taste in her mouth. "But he's also loyal."

"He wasn't to you, was he?"

Tasha's heart stopped. "Nora…my relationship with Dad is complicated," she answered cautiously. "Why do you ask?"

Nora sighed. "Forget it. Listen, are you going to hang out here? Because I'm pretty wiped."

"Go ahead. I'll call you when I get news."

Nora did look tired, but Tasha sensed her disappointment. Sadness at being unable to share with Nora her past dampened the burgeoning closeness she'd felt between them.

The urge to offer something to ease that look from Nora's face had her opening her mouth, but Tasha controlled the impulse. She wouldn't burden Nora. It was bad enough for Natalie. Besides, they all had enough on their plate.

JOSH WALKED THROUGH the sliding double doors and immediately spied Tasha, sitting with her head in her hands, shoulders sagging. He didn't hesitate, knowing only that she felt incredibly alone.

She looked up just as he approached. Surprise melted into relief and she allowed him to gather her into his arms.

Wrapping her tighter, he willed some of his strength into her, instinctively knowing she was hanging by a thread.

As if remembering herself, Tasha pulled away first, her cheeks coloring. "How'd you know?" she asked.

"Nora called. Said you might need someone."

Her smile weak, Tasha could only nod. "She was right. I told my sisters to go home. Figured only one of us needed to be here."

"How's he doing?"

Tasha's bleak look went straight to his heart in a way that was entirely too powerful, and if it weren't for Tasha's forced attempt at keeping distance between them, he would've pulled her to his chest to stay. "The doctor hasn't come back yet. You didn't need to come. I'm fine."

"Tasha, there's no need to put up a front for me. Okay? I know you better than most," he said quietly. She didn't disagree. "I'm here as long as you need me."

She swallowed and her voice came out in a hoarse whisper. "Thank you, Josh."

He took a seat beside her and they waited. After an hour, he felt Tasha lean against him in a subtle movement. Before long, her head lolled on his shoulder. She was asleep.

Josh took a long moment gazing down at her. Her delicate profile took him back in time to when she used to lean into him in the darkened movie theater. Her head resting comfortably against his bicep as if the muscle of his arm was created for that purpose. He smothered the spark in his heart, ashamed at how much he craved her. He had no right trying to relive the past. His feelings were still tangled and bitter over his divorce. And he was still reeling from her revelation earlier. They'd had their moment—they were two very different people now.

The doctor entered and Josh gently nudged Tasha. "Doc's back, sweetheart," he said, unable to resist the endearment.

Tasha blinked and hastily rubbed at her eyes, fully alert and anxious. "My dad…how is he?"

The doctor gave her a reassuring smile, though his words were grave. "Your father is a lucky man. By all accounts he should be dead. We were able to repair the damage with a triple bypass. He's in recovery. Why don't you go home and get some rest. You can see him in the morning."

Tasha nodded and the doctor left, but Josh could tell she really wanted to see her dad. Her concern was etched on her face. Josh put a hand on her shoulder and gently squeezed. "The doc's right. Let me drive you to your hotel."

"That's not necessary. I have my car," she said, turning with a shy smile. "But thank you for coming. It meant a lot to have you here."

"There's no place I'd rather be," he said. "You sure you don't want me to drive? You can always have your sisters bring your car back."

She looked tempted, and that slight hesitation made him want to insist, but in light of his new knowledge, he simply waited.

"I don't want to put my sisters out. They're dealing with enough as it is. I don't want them to feel like they're my chauffeur."

He doubted they'd feel that way, but he wasn't going to press it. It was enough that her feelings had been sincere the moment he came through the door. He walked her to the entrance. "Call me if you need anything."

She nodded but remained silent. There was a wall between them, and while he should've taken that as a sure sign to back off, it just made him ache all the more for the pain she was determined to face alone.

Grinding his jaw with frustration at his inability to reach out to her in a way she would welcome, he watched as she walked out the door.

CHAPTER SIXTEEN

TASHA ROSE EARLY THE NEXT morning, her head fuzzy from lack of true sleep, and quickly showered and dressed. She made phone calls to her sisters and then headed out.

Grabbing a coffee at the Roasting Company, she drove the short distance to the hospital and went straight to her father's room.

He was awake and looked far better, despite the tubes winding in and out of his body, and relief made her eyes water.

"Don't start the waterworks," her father's gruff voice said as she came to the side of his bed. "If people would stop poking and prodding at me I'd be just fine."

Tasha smiled through her tears. "I bet your nurses are drawing straws to see who puts the pillow over your face when you sleep."

Gerald tried to chuckle, but he winced and stiffened. "Well, I'm ready to get out of here. Hospitals are for sick people," he groused.

"Just sit tight. I'm not about to take you home and have you keel over again. I think one traumatic event in one week is sufficient." She sat beside him. "So, other than being your grouchy self, how do you feel?"

"Sore."

"You know what this means…"

He cast her a suspicious look. "What?"

"You're going to stick to the meal plans Natalie has taken the time to create for your stubborn ass." He started to grumble but Tasha wasn't hearing it. "Listen, Dad. You're all we've got. Mom didn't have a choice in how she went out, but you've being given a second chance at life. You can beat this with good eating habits and regular exercise." She waited a beat, then said in earnest, "We need you, Dad."

"Need you…" Gerald repeated softly. His expression faltered and his eyes clouded in a way that immediately had her reaching for the call button, but he stayed her hand. When she looked at him again, his eyes had cleared and resolution shone back at her. She frowned. "Dad? Are you okay?"

For the first time in a long time, Tasha caught a glimpse of the man she'd grown up thinking of as her hero. She sucked in a sharp breath. "Daddy? What's gotten into you? Are you sure you're all right?"

Tears sparkled in his eyes and he grasped her hand. "Not quite. But I will be. Someone made me promise and I aim to keep it."

A FEW DAYS LATER GERALD WAS released with strict dietary and medical instructions that made Tasha's head spin and Nora's eyes glaze, but Natalie didn't so much as blink as she jotted down the instructions. Tasha felt a momentary flash of guilt as she figured she should be the one to shoulder the bulk of the responsibility, but honestly, Natalie seemed like such a pro, Tasha wasn't about to step in unless asked.

And, Natalie didn't. In fact, she told Tasha to get out and relax for the day. She didn't say "why don't you call up, Josh," but somehow the suggestion lingered between them.

At first, she thought to head to the library to e-mail her director, but Tasha knew if she started composing the e-mail she'd sense what was coming and break down and cry.

She wasn't ready to leave—and that scared the holy living shit out of her.

And, it wasn't just because of her father's health, she knew. It was Josh.

Damn it. How'd this happen? Very quickly, she

noted wryly even as she locked her hotel door and headed for her car.

But being cognizant of your actions doesn't always mean you have the willpower to stop them, and that's exactly where Tasha was in her mind. She wanted to see Josh. Plain and simple. There, it was out there. Now what?

She craved his presence, if only offered in friendship. He knew her awful secret, there was nothing else she had to hide. And she knew what she needed. Tasha wasted no time in heading straight for Josh's house. Hopefully, he liked surprises.

JOSH WISHED DEAN HAD LINED up some work for him. He was going stir-crazy at home. He'd run out of projects on the small house, which didn't require a major overhaul—it was a rental, after all— and he was never much of a television watcher. Nor was he a reader. So that left doing a lot of thinking.

Of course, his thoughts were decidedly one-track. All of Tasha in varying degrees of appropriateness. Her smile, her skin, the smell of her hair, the way her expressive eyes held a wealth of sadness…everything about her wound his insides tight. He wanted to beat the shit out of whoever had hurt her when she was a young woman and he wanted to hold her close when she cried. *Knock it off, already!* Springing from the sofa as if it were on fire, he headed for the garage until a soft knock stopped him.

He crossed to the door and opened it, expecting to see Jehovah's Witnesses or Mormons hoping to convert him, when he saw Tasha looking like a manifestation of his thoughts.

"My sisters practically threw me out, saying I needed to take a day and relax and…well, you're the first person I thought of that I'd like to spend the day with. Is that okay?"

His heart thundered in his chest and he smiled through the breathlessness he felt, not about to turn her away no matter how much better for the both of them it would be. "Come in."

His small house wasn't dirty, but it definitely looked lived-in by two resident males. Crossing to the sofa, he pulled one of Christopher's dirty socks from the top and tossed it toward his son's room.

"Don't clean up on my account," she said with a self-deprecating laugh. "At least you have carpet, not a dirt floor."

She had a point, he thought. Remembering his manners, he headed toward the kitchen. "Can I get you something? I have some fresh-brewed coffee."

"I'd love a cup."

Tasha took a seat on the sofa and Josh disappeared

into the kitchen. When he returned with two cups, Tasha was looking at a picture of Christopher.

"He was about eight there," Josh offered, handing her the mug. "It's my favorite. And about the only picture Carrie let me have when we split."

"He looks so much like you in this picture," she said, accepting the mug, looking up at him with heartbreaking sincerity. "Seeing you as a father makes me wish things had been different between us," she admitted, dropping her gaze to the coffee cup. "That things had ended differently."

He let his gaze caress her face and believed in his heart if fate hadn't been so cruel, she would've been a wonderful mother. He swallowed with difficulty, unable to put into words what he felt in his heart but needed to squelch. She looked up in time to catch the struggle.

"What's wrong?" she asked. "You've got a funny look on your face."

"Tasha…" He choked down his words, hating the questions in his head and knowing she didn't want to answer them. He didn't blame her, but it didn't stop his need to know. Josh shook his head and cleared his mind. "Want to go for a ride?"

TASHA BLINKED IN SURPRISE at his sudden offer. "Where?"

"Don't care. Coulterville, Greeley Hill… Oakhurst, Fish Camp…I don't care. Let's just get out of the house."

"It's supposed to rain later today," she said with a flare of uncertainty, though excitement had ignited in her stomach. An impromptu road trip fit perfectly within her current reckless frame of mind. Suddenly, a picture materialized in her head and she bit her lip against the urge to identify it. A wildness she hadn't felt in ages took hold and she sent Josh a slow smile. "How about your parents' place in Wawona?"

Josh stared, a myriad of emotions floating across his features, until he matched her smile. "Wawona it is. I hope you packed something warm, because if it's raining here it'll snow there."

Tasha laughed. "Let's hit the road. I want to get there before noon."

THE RIDE TO WAWONA, MUCH like the ride to Yosemite, was achingly beautiful despite the cold, and little patches of snow provided crystalline flashes of brilliant color when the sun hit it just right. The dense forest flanking the road on both sides made Tasha feel at home, having made this trip more times than she could count in her childhood.

Rain clouds hovered, but the sun fought a gallant

battle to keep them at bay for a few more hours and Tasha was grateful for the brief window of sunshine.

Within an hour they pulled into the driveway, Josh's wide truck tires crunching on the frozen ground, alerting the wildlife to their presence. Tasha jumped out of the truck and inhaled the fresh smell of the forest that surrounded them.

The house, an odd, sprawling one-story, was built in the early 1900s and had been passed down through the Halvorsen generations. It was nearly impossible to find property in Wawona anymore, which made the place even more valuable.

It wasn't beautiful; in fact, the house was in need of repair, but each brother spent weeks every summer working on one project after another. Josh explained during the ride that he and Dean had renovated the bathroom, which had been a nightmare with the anti-quated plumbing.

Tasha spun in a slow circle. There were no mani-cured lawns, no evidence of man's heavy touch, just a rickety fence that failed to keep out the deer and a few seasonal neighbors who shared the same love of the area.

"It's not the Hilton—" Josh started to say, but Tasha turned with a warm smile.

"It's better," she finished for him, her breath visible before her as her cheeks started to sting from the cold. "There's no place better than here."

"Let's get inside before we freeze," he said, chuckling, leading her to the door, his hand resting lightly on the small of her back. Tasha felt the warmth of his hand despite the layers of clothing she wore and she was tempted to lean into him. Josh removed the temptation when he maneuvered around her to unlock the door. "After you," he said, eliciting a laugh from Tasha. "I'm going to get some firewood out of the wood cellar. Make yourself comfortable."

Tasha wandered into the living room, delighting in the antique furniture and aged smell of the house. A long table was situated in the formal dining room and three old-fashioned, single-hung wooden windows faced the backyard. Memories of card games, Monopoly tournaments and even a naughty game or two of strip poker when she and Josh came up alone, filled her mind. A subtle heat crawled into her cheeks and she touched them just to be sure she wasn't heating up the room. Still, there were many good memories in this old house and her heart was light.

Josh returned with an armful of seasoned wood and set to building a fire. Tasha watched with unabashed interest. There was something intensely masculine about a man doing something that at one time in their ancestry was essential to survival. Primal. She swallowed with difficulty. Somewhere in the back of her mind a voice weakly told her to stop where she was going, but she'd lost the will-power to listen. Josh turned, but when he read the heady desire in her eyes, his own darkened and he seemed to be fighting the same fight.

"Josh…" she said softly. What was there to say? She craved him in a way that was nonsensical and reckless, but it had slowly become a hunger inside her that only he could satisfy. He rose slowly and her heartbeat quickened. In a dark, reserved place in her mind, she'd known there was only one reason she'd suggested this place and Josh had known, as well. She sensed his reluctance, but his body responded to hers, and within moments he was standing close enough to touch. And that's what she did. As if touch-ing him for the first time, she caressed the side of his cheek and his eyelids shut briefly, almost painfully. She meant to etch this moment in her memory, for she knew it was a one-time deal. Staring into his eyes, she said, "Give me something I can cherish, Josh."

FOR ONCE, THE CHATTER IN Josh's head stilled and all that existed was the feel of Tasha in his arms. It felt so natural, so right. He pulled her against him, her body fitting into the grooves of his own as if they were made for each other. "Tasha..."

She quieted him with a soft, gentle, exploratory kiss that made his knees buckle with its sweetness, and whatever he'd been trying to say drowned in the swirl of desire that matched hers. Tasha led him to the first bedroom, to the bed where she lost her virginity to this same man, and knew by the flare in his eyes, he was remembering that night, as well.

The room was cold, the heat from the fire had only just started to warm the house, but Tasha tore her sweater from her body and encouraged Josh to do the same as she devoured him with her eyes. His body was different than she remembered, harder and more mature, but the changes excited her in a way she'd never allowed herself to experience. After Bronson, anything sexual had shamed her. But not with Josh. She felt safe enough to allow desire to run free in her body and she was excited by its power.

Josh came behind her and slid the straps of her bra down her shoulders, baring the soft skin to his lips. He cupped her full breasts and her head fell back, exposing the column of her neck. Chills tingled through her as he lightly nipped at the sensitive skin, traveling to the delicate shell of her ear. Turning her gently, Josh eased her against multiple lacy pillows. The antique brass bed groaned and creaked as it took their weight. Josh crawled toward her with a feral expression shining from his beautiful eyes, which stopped her heart in a painfully exciting way. This man was going to brand her with his lovemaking, she realized. He was going to sear away every foul memory. Tasha shuddered and offered her body and soul like never before.

JOSH'S MIND CEASED working. All that mattered was Tasha. Her smooth skin felt like hot satin against his body, and it was all he could do not to plunge into her like the young kid he used to be. Hands shaking, he touched her body reverently, the craving inside him almost too much to bear. Her eyelids fluttered shut and a moan escaped as he slipped a finger deep inside her. Dipping down, he claimed her nipple even as he worked his finger, slowly and gently, teasing the tight nub inside her hot folds until she writhed beneath him.

"Josh," she cried, clutching at his shoulders. "Please…"

Her gasped plea only encouraged him to take her closer to the brink without allowing that final completion. But as he positioned his body, she stiffened. His gaze flew to hers and he read the fear, even though she tried to hide it. Cupping her face gently, he kissed her long and deep, reminding her that it was him and he was not taking but giving. She inhaled sharply as if swallowing a sob and relaxed. Her arms tightened around him and he slowly entered her body, each stroke deliberate and unhurried, communicating with his actions he truly did cherish her and the gift she was offering.

CHAPTER SEVENTEEN

CURLED NAKED AGAINST JOSH, Tasha felt her heart hammer in her chest with the same wild beat as his, and she smiled, stretching and turning so that she was on her back and able to look at him.

His eyes opened and for a long moment just held her gaze. They'd poured their feelings into their bodies, allowing touch to communicate what they couldn't say out loud, and Tasha didn't expect words. Josh grazed her lips and slid his free hand across her belly, pulling her close.

"Tasha, what does this mean?"

His question made her sad. To answer *nothing* would cheapen what she'd considered profound, but to hope or pretend that there could be more between them was unfair to them both. "You know it's not that simple," she said.

He nodded grimly. "I know."

"Wrong time for us again, I guess," she said.

"It doesn't have to be."

She sighed, wishing he'd let it go. But she could tell by the determined set of his jaw, she'd have to explain why. "I'm not the person people remember. When you grow up in a small town everyone expects you to stay the same, like some cookie cut-out, always smiling and waving from the sidelines. I'm not that cheerleader anymore."

"I think you're wrong. No one expects people to remain the same. Emmett's Mill is not Pleasantville."

Tasha gave Josh a derisive look. "Isn't it? Every person I've run into has brought up how I'd once been the prom queen and how I haven't changed a bit. They're wrong. I've changed so much I'm damn near unrecognizable, and frankly, I'm not interested in telling them why."

Understanding crossed his features, but she didn't want his understanding or sympathy. She wanted to be left alone. Pulling from his arms, she slid from the bed and began dressing. "Josh, I've spent years wondering how I could possibly manage to move back to Emmett's Mill, but each time I consider the possibility I think of the chance that I might run into his wife. She's a living reminder of what happened and she believed him. Not that I blame her entirely. Why would she believe something so hideous of her husband? A man respected in the community and his church? No. Invariably, I come back around to the same conclusion. Emmett's Mill is not my home any longer."

Josh followed, grabbing his jeans from the floor just as she donned her sweater. "Running isn't the answer," he said.

His tone wasn't self-righteous but Tasha couldn't help but bristle. He had no idea what it was like to live in her skin. "It worked for you," she said quietly, referencing their ugly breakup so many years ago.

Josh stilled. The moment was all but ruined between them. Regretful for her harsh words, she reached out to him, but there was no warmth in his eyes to encourage her touch. She dropped her arm. "We can't have forever. It's not meant to be. Let's be content with the moment. Okay?"

"Impossible," he muttered, shoving his hand through his hair as he stalked from the room.

Straightening the bed covers, she gathered the rest of her things and reluctantly followed. She found Josh staring out the window toward the backyard, watching as the sky darkened with the threat of snow.

"We should get back before that storm hits," she

said, thinking of Christopher. "Those clouds look like they mean business."

He nodded but he didn't move.

"Josh—"

"Tell me his name."

Tasha startled. "Excuse me?"

He turned to her. "I want to know his name."

Tasha started to protest, to explain again how knowing a dead man's identity wasn't going to change anything, but somehow she found her lips moving in a different way than she'd desired and honesty flowed from her mouth. "Bronson Lewis."

Josh's eyes widened as if he didn't believe it, and she flinched inside, waiting for the evidence of his disbelief.

"Son of a bitch," he whispered. "I knew that bastard wasn't right in the head."

Tasha's knees weakened for a moment as she moved toward him. "What do you mean?" she asked in a stricken voice. Had Josh seen something that tipped him off, some sign that she'd obviously missed?

"Nothing I can put my finger on, but there was something creepy about the way he…leered at girls half his age." When Tasha couldn't do anything but stare, he shook his head as if at himself for not saying anything sooner. "My dad never thought much of him, either. He said he never knew what Diane saw in the bastard. And, I think my dad's one of the best judges of characters there is, so if he didn't like him, the guy already started with one point against him. When I caught him chatting up Leanne Stillman one day after practice, it made me sick. There was no mistaking what he was after that day."

Tasha felt sick herself. Bronson had been a fixture at the high school because he volunteered as an assistant coach for the varsity football team, among other things. She'd never given his presence at the school a second thought, not to mention he was such a good friend of her dad's. Her hand went to her stomach even as she sank into the nearest chair.

Josh came to kneel beside her, all trace of anger gone. "If I'd known you were working for him I'd have told you to steer clear. I'd have least told you to watch out."

Tasha buried her face in her hands. "How could I have been so blind? Why didn't I see it?"

"Because he was a manipulative bastard and accomplished liar. I mean, c'mon, the guy was a lawyer. They don't make jokes about lawyers for nothing."

Tasha lifted her head to give Josh a derisive look. "Not all lawyers are bad," she said, sighing. "Although, as you're just coming off a divorce, I'm sure your opinion of them isn't very high."

"The point is, he was a predator, and honestly, Tasha…there's no telling how many other young women he victimized."

"I think he hurt Chloe," she whispered, voicing her secret fear.

Josh stared long and hard and she could see the revulsion crossing his features. "Why do you say that?"

"Gut instinct," she said. "Maybe some kind of victim sixth sense. I don't know. But it's there and I don't doubt it."

"Then I don't doubt it, either," he said, his voice grim. "Maybe you should talk with Chloe, try to help her."

She despised the idea that perhaps her silence had allowed him to hurt Chloe, but she couldn't face the woman. She swallowed the panic burgeoning in her throat, secure in the knowledge that the hated man was dead and there would be no more victims of Bronson Lewis.

"What good will that do?" she asked, averting her gaze. "It's in the past. Just let it go."

"Let it go? This is something you need to deal with. A horrible thing happened to you, but don't let it define who you are."

She regarded him coldly. "Drop it, Josh. I mean it."

"And if I don't?"

Her chest tightened as she regarded him with true sadness. Her voice clear and without reservation, she said, "Then, this time the one who's running me out of Emmett's Mill…is you."

THE RIDE BACK TO TOWN was silent and fraught with tension. Josh knew Tasha hadn't said what she did for effect. Tasha had never been one to indulge in petty drama. But he couldn't understand her not wanting to help Chloe. Because he was sure that in helping the young woman Tasha would help herself. Maybe she'd forgive herself.

One glance at Tasha and his gut roiled all over again. Why, Tasha? Why won't you fight?

Soon, he pulled into Tasha's hotel parking lot and let the truck idle. He went to get out but she laid a hand on his shoulder.

"Please don't be disappointed in my decision," she pleaded, but he couldn't help himself. "I've had to live with this for almost thirteen years and I've found a way to do that. I can't start all over. It'll kill me."

"You wouldn't be alone," he insisted softly, bringing his hand to lightly touch her jaw. "I promise."

Tasha placed her hand atop his and her eyelids fluttered shut for the briefest moment, but when she opened them, she pulled his hand from her face. "That's not a promise you can make and one I'd never hold you to."

"Tasha—" he started, but she'd already opened the door and jumped out. Staring after her, he wondered if she was right. Maybe it was best to leave it alone. Maybe it was best for her to leave.

At the thought of watching Tasha walk out of his life again, his future looked very bleak. After today, he realized he'd been stumbling through life, moving from one experience to another in an endless gray calendar, broken only by the colorful joy his son brought, and he didn't want to go back to that life.

But what choice did he have? When she left, he knew his heart might just go with her.

CHAPTER EIGHTEEN

CHRISTOPHER'S HANDS WERE shaking. A text message from OgDog had liquefied the contents of his lower intestine and he was freaking out.

He glanced down at his cell and reread the message, wishing there was a different way to interpret it.

Dump all codes. Wash mainframe. ASAP.

He swallowed the growing fear and started moving. He knew of a few ways to sanitize a hard drive, but he also knew if someone found out he and Og had accessed Zodiac's mainframe and the bigwigs called the feds, they'd have some IT geek who could resurrect any washed file or activity. Wiping at the sweat popping along his brow, he prayed somehow he and Og had slipped under the radar. It was just a game, he wanted to shout, but fear kept him quiet. His dad was going to blow a gasket and his grandfather…

well, he wouldn't put it past the old man to take a switch to his ass.

This kind of shit doesn't really happen except in the movies, he told himself, even as he gathered every scrap of paper that had any kind of reference to the Zodiac game and tossed it into the fireplace to burn.

He returned to his room at a sprint and hit the necessary combination to bleach the hard drive of the computer he used to play the Zodiac game.

His dad was due home any minute. Christopher was working against the clock and his computer seemed to be taking forever to get the job done. *C'mon, already!*

Christopher heard tires crunch on the gravel driveway and he swore. His dad was home early.

He ran and tossed more paperwork into the fireplace when a knock at the front door had him skidding to a stop. Fear trickled down his back and he considered hiding in his room. The knock sounded again, this time more insistent.

"Just a minute," he called out, his voice cracking. He padded to the door and opened it reluctantly. Two men dressed in identical suits stared at him with stern expressions and Christopher knew federal agents were assessing him.

"Christopher Angelus Halvorsen?"

He couldn't find his voice so he nodded instead.

"You're under arrest for hacking into and obtaining restricted, proprietary gaming information from Zodiac Games, which has resulted in a level-one security breach."

Christopher found his voice. "I want to call my dad."

JOSH WAS JUST GETTING off work when his cell phone rang. When he saw it was Chris, he answered immediately.

"Dad? I'm in big trouble," Christopher said, his voice wavering in a way that reminded Josh of when he was small.

"What's wrong? Are you okay?" he asked, but as Christopher started to answer the line was taken from him and a stranger answered.

"Mr. Halvorsen, your son is being arrested on federal hacking charges. We'll be detaining him at the local police station for the time being. Meet us there."

"What the hell are you talking about? You've got the wrong kid!" He shoved his hand through his hair. *Damn it, Chris.* He tried calming, but fear kept his voice harsh. "Christopher is a good boy. He'd never do what you're saying. You don't know him."

"Mr. Halvorsen, we have no doubt it was Christopher. His accomplice provided the information. Perhaps you don't know your son as well as you thought. See you soon, Mr. Halvorsen."

The line went dead and Josh stared at the phone in shock, not quite sure where to start. Carrie's accusatory tone echoed in his memory and guilt flooded his thoughts. Had he been too lenient? Too unobservant of his son's actions? He didn't want to think his son capable of breaking the law, but a sinking feeling told him he was wrong and he could barely put the keys into the ignition for his nerves. He fumbled with his cell phone, knowing he should call Carrie but dreaded it. His jaw set, he dialed his ex-wife's cell phone and prepared for the worst, determined to get it over with so he could focus on Christopher before she arrived.

God, it burned like hell to know she'd been right.

Perhaps he wasn't as good a father as he thought. The sting of that went deep, and for the first time ever, he wondered if he'd made the right decision bringing Christopher here instead of toughing it out at his old school.

Carrie picked up the line.

Not wishing to drag this out, he kept it short and sweet. "Chris is in some kind of trouble. I don't know what's going on yet, I'm on my way to the police station to find out. I thought you might like to know."

"Should I drive up?" she asked, the concern in her voice taking him by surprise. "I could be there in about an hour and a half."

"Uh, no, why don't you wait until I figure out what's happened. It could be a big misunderstanding." God, he could only hope.

"What's it about?" she asked before he could disconnect.

He hesitated but knew she'd find out sooner or later. "Something to do with computers," he admitted, feeling her judgment from across the phone line. "I'm sure it's a misunderstanding."

She seemed to sense his tension and chose not to pick a fight. "Let me know when you find out. I'll wait for your call."

He agreed, and the moment the line went dead, his fingers were dialing Tasha, though he didn't know what he expected from her. They hadn't spoken since the Wawona trip, though not because she wasn't on his mind. He just didn't know what to say that wouldn't make things worse. He'd never been a smooth talker and Tasha knew that about him, but right now he was wishing he had some of Sammy's skill because he needed her and wasn't ashamed to admit he was scared. When she answered on the second ring, he said, "Tasha, it's me. I need you."

"Josh?" she answered, immediately knowing something was wrong. "Are you all right? You sound shook up."

"It's Christopher…I don't know what's going on but he's been arrested by the feds. They're holding him at the local police station. They said something about hacking."

"Hacking? Oh, no…did they say anything else?"

"No, just that I had to come to the station."

"All right, then that's what you need to do. It's going to be okay. Just keep your head straight so you can think. Christopher needs you to be the level head in there."

Tasha's voice soothed the tightness building in his chest and he drew a deep breath. "Thank you," he said. "I know I shouldn't have called but…"

"Josh, stop. You can always call me. Would you like me to meet you at the station?"

"Yes," he said, refusing to feel badly about answering honestly. "I'd really appreciate that."

"I can be there in about ten minutes."

They said goodbye and he circled wide to pull onto the highway toward town. Knowing Tasha would be there with him settled his overactive brain and quieted the fear so that he could think clearly for the first moment since receiving the call.

Hacking? He thought of his conversation with Carrie about Chris's rampant computer use and he cringed. Carrie had been right. How had he been so blind?

TASHA PULLED INTO THE police station and Josh followed seconds later. He jumped from his truck and they walked in together.

Josh strode to the receiving window. "My son Christopher Halvorsen was just brought in."

The woman behind the glass perked up. "Your kid's the one with the feds, right?"

Josh ground his teeth. "That's what I've been told. Can I see him, please?"

"One minute. It's not often this town sees this kind of action."

Tasha squeezed his hand in silent support and he drew a deep breath. The woman buzzed them through and led them to a waiting room. They weren't there long before an austere man joined them.

"Mr. and Mrs. Halvorsen. I'm federal agent Phillip Malone." Tasha opened her mouth to correct his assumption but the agent didn't give her the chance. "Your son is in some serious trouble. Zodiac Games is a major corporation and they're not too happy right now with your son and his friend Paul."

Josh paled and Tasha sent him an encouraging smile. "I don't quite understand. Don't big companies like Zodiac have security to prevent these kinds of things? I don't understand how a teenager could do what you're saying," Josh said, shooting an uncertain look at Tasha. "He's only fourteen."

Malone shifted. "Your son has advanced computer skills. I'd say he's fairly gifted. Have you ever had his IQ tested?"

Josh shook his head and Tasha felt his confusion.

"It's a shame he used his brains to do something illegal."

"I'm sure he didn't mean to break the law," Josh protested. "Surely, there's someone we could talk to from Zodiac to get them to see that. I mean, he just likes to play that game."

"Hacking is considered cyber terrorism, Mr. Halvorsen. It may have seemed like just a game, but your son and his friend managed to break into a restricted area of the company mainframe to access the newest Zodiac game before it's even been released. These gaming companies take this *very* seriously."

"So what's next?" Tasha asked, giving Josh's hand another gentle squeeze.

"We're in contact with Zodiac's lawyers to see if they want to press charges, which I'm sure they will, and then we'll have to book him."

Josh swallowed. "Book him?"

"Sorry. Procedure." The agent looked genuinely apologetic. Maybe he had a kid, too, and could relate to Josh's pain. "We'll bring Christopher in and you can talk for a few minutes."

The agent left the room and Tasha turned to Josh. "Is Carrie on her way?"

He looked miserable. "She's waiting for my call. I told her I'd let her know if it was something serious. I was hoping to be able to tell her that it was nothing."

Tasha rose but he grasped her hand to stop her. "Please don't go," he said.

"I was just going to give you some privacy so you could call Carrie back. I won't go far," she promised. "But I think you need to tell her so she can decide how she wants to handle this."

Josh looked conflicted. "I know, but I'll call her later after we've figured out a few things. I would like you to stay…if you don't mind?"

The vulnerable expression on Josh's face squeezed her heart. How could she say no? He needed her and he was openly asking for her help. "Of course I'll stay. That's what friends are for."

"Tasha…you're so much more than my friend… and you probably always will be no matter what happens between us," he said quietly, taking her breath away. The door opened and Christopher walked in, wearing handcuffs and looking frightened.

"Dad…I'm so sorry," Christopher said, his mouth quivering. "What I did was so stupid."

Josh crossed to his son and wrapped the boy in a tight hug, kissing the top of his head without reservation. "We're going to figure this out. The key is to cooperate in any way possible. I'm sure the judge will take into consideration the fact this is your first offense. They're not going to put you in a cell and throw away the key," he said, though Tasha could hear the thread of fear in his voice.

She piped in. "Your dad's right. You're a good kid, Chris. I'm sure the judge will weigh that against the crime."

Josh regarded his son with a mixture of pain and confusion. "Why, Chris? Why would you do something like this? You had to know it wasn't right."

Christopher hung his head. "I really wanted to play the new game, and when Paul said he'd cracked the mainframe I figured the risk was minimal. Plus Paul seemed pretty confident we wouldn't get caught."

"But even if you hadn't been caught it was still illegal. Chris…basically you stole from this company."

"I know, Dad."

Josh exhaled. "All right…is there anything else I

should know about? What other systems have you hacked into?"

Christopher seemed affronted by the question. "Jeez, Dad, I only accessed Zodiac's system. I just wanted to see if their new game was worth all the hype."

Tasha couldn't resist. "Was it?"

Josh shot Tasha a warning look, but Christopher cracked a sheepish grin. "Until I got caught? Yeah. But now, not so much."

Tasha gave Josh a reassuring smile, but he wasn't warming to it. She tried again. "I think the lesson's been learned. What do you think, Chris?"

Christopher looked unhappy but he nodded.

"It's not that simple," Josh said sharply, but she didn't take offense. "Chris…you might not walk away from this. Damn it, they might put you in a juvenile lockup or take you out of my custody. Did you think of any of that before you did something so rash? So *irresponsible?*"

"Josh…" Tasha said in a soothing voice, seeing Christopher tremble and knowing how bad the kid must be feeling to disappoint his father so much. "Let's think positively. Like you said, he's a first-time offender. Surely, there's room for a little leniency."

"What if there isn't? What if they try to make an example out of my kid?"

She bit her lip and shook her head. There were no guarantees. That worst-case scenario could happen. She hoped to God it didn't.

"I'm sorry, Dad," Christopher said, sniffling back his tears and looking younger than his fourteen years. "I won't do it again. I swear."

Josh dragged his palms down his face and eyed his son with a mixture of disappointment and pain. "I want to believe you. I do," he said, his voice breaking. "I'm going to have to call your mom. She's waiting to find out what happened."

Christopher nodded glumly. "I guess. She'll just yell at me."

"You deserve it," Josh said.

"Yeah, I know."

Agent Malone returned and unhooked the handcuffs. "It's as I thought, they want to press charges. We've booked him, but since he's a juvenile and not what we consider a flight risk, we'll release him into your custody." As Malone continued, Josh's relief was short-lived. "He is not to leave the county or the state. Your son is in a lot of trouble. Do everyone a favor and don't let him make it worse. His court date will be in a few days."

Christopher rubbed his wrists, asking, "What happened to my friend, Paul?"

Malone stared at Christopher, his gaze only a little sympathetic as he answered, "He's not your friend, son. According to him you were the mastermind, collecting the codes and giving them to him instead of the other way around." Christopher's eyes widened in shock. "Yeah, lucky for you, your friend has a prior working against him. You're smart, no doubt about it, but it's clear Paul was the one who cracked the code. In the future, you might want to pick better friends." This was directed at Christopher, but Josh felt the reprimand, as well. If he'd been more observant of his son's friends maybe this wouldn't have happened. He was so busy ignoring anything that came out of Carrie's mouth from pure bitterness that he'd missed something crucial.

Malone departed and they were free to leave—for now.

"Someone will be in touch within a day or two," the woman behind the glass counter said.

Once outside, Josh turned to Tasha, looking shaken but still trying to hold it together. "That really sucked," he said, trying for the irreverent levity

Sammy wielded like an art form. Unfortunately, Josh wasn't the joker in the family and the flat landing only accentuated the worry in his voice. Christopher walked away to stand beside the truck, his shame and embarrassment evident in his posture.

Tasha's heart went out to the boy. She placed a hand on Josh's shoulder, saying softly so Chris didn't overhear, "I know you're disappointed, but try to remember that he's just a kid and right now he needs you. He's scared, too."

Josh nodded. "I know. I'm trying to keep sight of that. It's hard, though. I can't believe I was so blind. I should've seen something was up. God, I should've paid better attention."

Tasha frowned. "You need to be strong. Don't waste the energy beating yourself up for something you couldn't control."

Josh angled a sardonic look at her. "Good advice. But hard to follow, isn't it?"

She sucked in a sharp breath, seeing his point. Her cheeks flared. "We're not talking about me," she said in a low voice. "My situation doesn't even compare to this one. Besides you need to focus on how you're going to get your son through this crisis. That's all that matters."

"I know." Josh sighed. "Thank you for staying. I've never felt so…out of place. Chris is a good kid. This is the first time I've had to deal with that sort of thing. The last time we were at a police station was when that kid assaulted him."

Tasha inhaled the subtle yet comforting scent that clung to his sweatshirt and nodded. It was such a natural thing to stand beside him. Sobering, she said, "You should call Carrie," but the reminder was unnecessary. Carrie was walking toward them, her expression stiff.

"I thought you said you were going to wait for my phone call," Josh said, irritation lacing his tone. "You've wasted a trip. There's nothing that can be done right now."

Tasha tried to move away but Josh grasped her hand and held it firmly, as if making a statement to his ex-wife. Tasha sent an unsure glance at Josh, but he was preparing for the battle ahead and she could feel him tensing.

"I changed my mind," Carrie answered, her gaze sliding to Tasha with open hostility. "He's *my* son, and even if I could only see him for a minute, I wanted him to know I'm here for him."

"I'm fine, Mom," Christopher said glumly, accepting a brief hug. "I have to wait a few days for my court appearance."

"Good, that gives us a chance to hire a good lawyer. In the meantime, you're coming home with me."

Josh jerked. "No, he's not."

If it hadn't been for Josh's strong grip she might've used that as her cue to leave. Tasha wasn't afraid of Carrie but she had enough on her plate. She didn't relish dealing with Carrie on top of everything else.

Carrie squared her shoulders, preparing for a fight. "I should tell you that this incident has made me reevaluate your ability to care for him full-time." Carrie's gaze narrowed. "Obviously, being in your physical custody isn't working out. At least when he's with me, I know he's not on the computer breaking the law."

"Mom…" Christopher interjected plaintively, but she wasn't listening, her focus was centered on Josh.

Josh's face reddened. "You're going a bit far, Carrie. How was I supposed to know he knew how to hack into a major company's computer?"

"Maybe if you weren't so busy trying to recreate the past, you'd have noticed Christopher's unhealthy fascination," Carrie said coolly, pointedly staring at Tasha.

"Well, you can't take him," Josh snapped. "He's not allowed to leave the county until his court date."

Tasha released Josh's hand. "You should do this in private," she said to Josh, moving away despite his protest.

"Thank you," Carrie said, though her eyes were wintry. "At least one of you knows when to do the right thing."

Tasha stopped and turned, not able to ignore that little dig at Josh's expense when he was clearly struggling with his own guilt about the situation. "Carrie, Josh is an excellent father. This could've happened to anyone. Don't use this incident to punish him. It's not right. Deep in your heart, you know that, too," she said, trying to appeal to Carrie's sense of compassion.

But Carrie merely offered a smile that clearly said, Back the hell out of my business, and Tasha decided to do just that.

"Sorry, Josh," she muttered, and left, despite wanting to set a few things straight with Carrie.

Carrie's spiteful comment held some truth. She'd always known trying to rekindle anything substantial with Josh was a mistake, but it was hard to ignore how good it felt to be around him. In a way, she should thank Carrie for jerking her back to reality.

As she pulled out of the police station parking lot, a glance in her rearview mirror revealed Carrie and Josh arguing heatedly. She felt the damp fingers of shame trailing down her back, but she stiffened against the emotion. This wasn't her fight. It was between Josh and Carrie. Her heart leaden inside her chest, she drove away, reminding herself it wasn't her place to play house with Josh. Christopher was Carrie's child—not hers.

JOSH WATCHED TASHA FADE from his peripheral vision and he cursed in the privacy of his mind while his mouth argued with Carrie.

"I didn't know where your misplaced judgment was coming from, but now it seems perfectly clear. I will not have you replacing me with her," Carrie said, her brown eyes hot with anger. "Anyone but *her.*"

"I'm not replacing you as Chris's mother," he assured her, but it rankled that she was drawing this line when she'd been cavalier about her involvement with Robert. He was a man Josh wholeheartedly distrusted, but he had no choice but to swallow his misgivings provided the man didn't lay a hand on Christopher. "But who I date is none of your business," he said quietly.

Carrie's mouth dropped open, but the hard, uncompromising stare he sent her made her reconsider. Unable to counter with anything, she exhaled unhappily.

"Why her?" she asked, her voice small and vulnerable. "Why couldn't it be anyone but her?"

"Because I love her," Josh admitted, knowing his admission only poured salt on the wound. "I'm sorry."

Carrie took a moment to compose herself, wiping at the corners of her eyes before her tears could destroy the carefully applied makeup on her eyes. She cleared her throat. "Robert knows quite a few influential people," she started, but Josh shook his head, not liking where she was heading. "Josh, this is serious. He could see jail time for this. Robert could make a few calls and get him off with a minor slap on the wrist and then we can all forget about this embarrassing event."

"No. Whatever he gets, he deserves. But I don't think the judge is going to throw the book at him. I think he'll probably get community service and probation on the condition that he keep his nose clean."

"You're willing to take that chance?" Carrie asked, scandalized. When Josh nodded grimly, she shook her head. "Well, I'm not. You can pin your hopes on a lenient judge, but I'm not going to watch my son go to jail for a stupid stunt that you should've been on top of. This is your fault. Just remember that while you're off playing with Natasha Simmons your only child is sitting out the rest of his teenage years in a locked-down facility surrounded by real criminals."

Josh's temper flared and something dangerous must've flashed in his blue eyes, for Carrie stiffened and turned on her heel. As she got to her car, her withering stare didn't bode well. "My lawyer will be in touch," she said, confirming his gut feeling.

"Of that…I have no doubt."

CHAPTER NINETEEN

TASHA SAT WITH HER SISTERS later that night, trying to stay focused on the present conversation without seeming distracted, but she must've been doing a lousy job because Nora called her on it.

"What's wrong?" Nora asked, point blank.

Tempted to just share with her sisters to gain some perspective, she wavered when she caught Natalie's sharp gaze. If she told them why she was with Josh down at the station, would that give away too much? Tasha chewed on her bottom lip. Natalie had an uncanny ability to see through her bullshit. Suddenly weary of her own secrets and knowing that somehow Natalie would find out, anyway, and quite possibly tell Nora, she leaned back in her chair and decided to spill the beans.

Starting with the impromptu trip to Wawona—and pointedly ignoring the delighted gasps from Nora—she finished with Christopher's shocking arrest.

"Holy cow," breathed Nora. "You really know how to spice up a day trip."

"So, what's going to happen to Christopher?" Natalie asked.

"I'm not sure. I hope they don't try to make an example out of him," Tasha answered.

"It's the luck of the draw," Nora said. "He could get off with a slap or they could make a huge deal out of it. I guess it all depends on how irate Zodiac is at their security breach. You know the suits aren't always big on heart."

"How's Josh holding up? That's got to be pretty upsetting knowing your son's in such serious trouble," Natalie said, pricking Tasha's conscience.

"I haven't called him since leaving the police station. It's not really my place. Besides, it seemed he and Carrie had a lot to talk about."

"By the sounds of it she was just attacking him," Nora said. "From what Sammy's told me of her, she wasn't the most forgiving person in the world. I don't think the Halvorsen family were crying buckets when Josh announced they were divorcing."

"Nora, that's not nice," Tasha admonished. "Josh took the divorce pretty hard. He's still trying to get through it."

Nora shrugged. "He's probably better off. But back to the part where you slept with him. What's up with that?"

Natalie rolled her eyes at Nora and Tasha blushed. Perhaps she'd been too quick to share. She tried brushing past that particular detail, but it was the one Nora was most interested in. Her gray eyes were practically dancing at the prospect of details. Tasha sighed. "We have a lot of history. It just felt right…at the moment. It was pretty irresponsible, actually. God, it was irresponsible."

She'd like to say if she could she'd take it back, but that would be a lie. Tasha would probably savor that memory for years to come, particularly when she returned to Belize and she had nothing but the mosquitoes to keep her company.

"So what does this mean?" Nora asked.

"Why does it have to mean anything?" Tasha said.

Nora looked to Natalie for reinforcements.

"I think you still have feelings for Josh and it's okay for you to explore them," Natalie said gently, to which Tasha felt the urge to roll her eyes. "You and Josh had something special and rare. Maybe you're soul mates."

"Nat, are you ovulating or something?" Tasha

joked, but Nat's comment sent a riot of goose bumps down her arm. "Don't read too much into things. I'll always care for Josh, but I've decided it's time to go back to Belize."

"Why?" Nora practically wailed, and Tasha could see her distress was genuine. She could imagine how disappointing it must feel to her youngest sister. She felt it, as well, but she couldn't stay. "Why do you have to go? I don't understand."

Tasha knew she didn't. Perhaps Natalie was right and it was time to tell Nora why. Only, it wasn't just her feelings for Josh that made it impossible to stay.

"Josh and I had our chance, but it's gone. Trying to recreate something from the past isn't healthy and it eventually writes over the good memories you have. I don't want to do that. You're right, once Josh and I shared something amazing and I want to cherish those memories, not ruin them with less-than-perfect new ones."

"So, Carrie's not running you off, you're running yourself off, is that what you're saying?" Nora asked.

Tasha stiffened. "No, I'm not saying that at all."

"Sounds like it to me."

Natalie shot Nora an uncertain look but added, "Tasha, why exactly are you leaving, then?"

"Because there's no place for me here. I can't just insert myself into someone else's family picture just because I want to. Josh needs to focus on Christopher, not me."

"Tasha, having someone to lean on when times get tough is one of the perks of being in love. If I didn't have Evan to be there after a hard day, I'd have lost my mind a long time ago. Did you ever consider the possibility that being together makes you both stronger?"

Tasha smiled but her heart was heavy. "When did you get so wise?" she asked, suffering through a sudden pang of loss at the knowledge she was going to leave. She'd miss her sisters.

"When did you get so stubborn?" Natalie countered, and they both grinned.

Nora snorted with an answer for them both. "Probably around the same time, because you both annoy the hell out of me."

Laughter pushed away the melancholy that followed at the thought of saying goodbye and she focused on soaking up every moment with her sisters, determined to fill her well to overflowing so she had plenty to draw from when she was alone again.

THE NEXT MORNING TASHA stared at her laptop and contemplated e-mailing her director. It was past time, but as she opened her e-mail account, she hesitated. She couldn't tell her director she was coming back unless she really was ready to commit. Groaning, she closed her laptop, resolving to sit down tonight and write that e-mail. At the moment, she needed to talk with Josh. It felt wrong not to check on Christopher and Josh. After the uncomfortable scene with Carrie, she'd resolved to keep her distance, but the idea of leaving Josh to deal with the situation alone smacked of cowardice.

At one time she'd been fearless. One person had destroyed that aspect of her personality. And she hadn't been alone. At least one other person was fighting the memories, drowning them with alcohol.

Tasha drew a deep breath and swallowed against the tight feeling. She knew there was something else she had to do before she could start the slow climb back to the person she used to be. Bronson was dead, but his victims still felt his hold. That was going to stop. By God, it was going to stop.

TASHA WAITED NERVOUSLY at the Lewis house, waiting for someone to answer the door. She could only hope Chloe was still there.

Diane opened the door and Tasha fought the urge to run. "Is Chloe still here?"

Diane nodded but didn't appear inclined to let Tasha in, saying, "She's not feeling well. Perhaps you could visit another time."

"I can't, Diane. There's something we need to talk about and I'm leaving Emmett's Mill soon. May I please speak with her?"

A surly voice at the top of the stairs yelled for aspirin and Diane's stiff composure gave way to distress. "Uh, it's not a good time, Tasha…."

"How much has she been drinking?"

"More than should be humanly possible. I don't know what's wrong with her. She's turned into an alcoholic, I'm afraid, but she won't listen to me."

Chloe appeared at the door and her red-rimmed eyes narrowed at Tasha. "My mom said you and your boyfriend brought me home the other night. That true?"

"You don't remember?"

"No." The flat tone of her voice told Tasha there were probably many nights she doesn't care to remember. "What are you doing here?"

"I came to talk with you."

"What is this? An intervention from my old babysitter?" she sneered, and Diane blanched at her rudeness.

"No. I have something to tell you and I think you need to hear it."

Subtly intrigued, Chloe pushed past her mother to step outside. "Let's walk," she suggested. Diane protested, her gaze darting to her neighbors' homes, and Chloe snorted. "We'll stay off the main road so none of your precious friends see me. Okay?"

Diane looked ashamed that her daughter had zeroed in on her fear but nodded before closing the door.

"So what's this about? My friggin' head feels like it's about to explode and this bright sunlight isn't helping."

Tasha drew a deep breath, knowing Chloe wasn't in the mood for pleasantries. "Listen, what I have to say is upsetting but something tells me you won't be surprised."

"So tell me."

Tasha opened her mouth to just level with Chloe, but the words dried up in her throat. Her heartbeat pounded in her chest and tears sprang to her eyes.

"You okay?" Chloe asked.

"Chloe…what kind of relationship did you share with your father?"

Chloe's gaze went from stricken to guarded. "Why?"

Tasha stopped and Chloe followed suit. She searched the woman's face, hating how much she'd changed from the inside out and wondering if they both carried the same scars. "Did he hurt you? Did he…" The tears ran down her cheeks. "Oh, God, I don't know how to ask…did he touch you inappropriately?"

Chloe stiffened and she seemed frozen. "Why are you asking me this?" she whispered, but her eyes were glazing. "My father…he was a good man. Everyone said so."

That was the clue Tasha needed. "You weren't the only one," she said, moving closer to Chloe but being careful not to crowd her. "Your father…he raped me when I was twenty-two."

Chloe stared as if unable to comprehend what Tasha had said, then her head started to slowly shake. "You? Why?"

"I don't know. He wasn't a good man."

"Why are you telling me this?"

Tasha inhaled deeply for strength. "Because I saw a piece of me in you the other night. You're killing yourself with drugs and alcohol to smother the memories. Every day I work myself to the bone trying to forget what he did to me, but it doesn't work. He doesn't deserve that kind of power. He's already taken so much."

"It was on my thirteenth birthday," Chloe said,

shocking Tasha. "He said I was a woman now and it was his job as a father to do it."

"He was a bastard, Chloe."

Chloe rubbed at her nose and swallowed. "I tried to tell my mom but I couldn't find the words. I would've thought that she might've noticed that I avoided being around him at all costs, but she didn't. The day he died was the best day of my life." Tasha swallowed. She'd felt the same. Chloe's expression hardened. "I left when I turned eighteen and haven't looked back. Until now. I didn't have anywhere else to go. I lost my job and couldn't pay the rent anymore. I had no choice but to come home. I hate it here."

"He's dead. He can't hurt anyone anymore." Tasha risked gently touching Chloe's arm. "You don't have to punish yourself. You did nothing wrong."

"Yeah, well, my life is ruined just the same. I'm not the person I used to be."

Me, neither. "But you can make the choice to change. To stand instead of fall. Do you understand?"

"Easy for you to say," Chloe said sourly, her gaze raking Tasha's body. "Something tells me *you* didn't sell yourself for another drink. Do you know how many men I've…?" She smirked. "Well, you get the idea."

Tasha swallowed a shudder. "You can turn your

life around. You were a smart girl in high school. You have what you need to start over."

Chloe's bleak gaze tore into Tasha's heart, but a part of her wondered if she gave that same look to Josh when he asked about their future. She pushed that thought aside and focused on Chloe, needing to feel this woman wasn't lost. "Your mom needs to know. She wants to help you. I can tell this is tearing her apart. Whatever your differences are, when she's gone anything you might've wanted to say will be too late. There are so many things I wanted to tell my mom but I lost that opportunity. Don't waste yours."

"She'll never believe me. She thinks he was a saint."

"Don't underestimate your mom," Tasha said, hoping she wasn't wrong. "Do you love her?"

Chloe paused, then answered hesitantly, "Yeah, I guess."

"Then don't waste the time you have left together. She'll come around. And—" she took a deep breath, preparing herself to follow through if need be "—if she doesn't readily believe you, call me. I'll tell her what happened to me. We'll make her see together."

"You'd do that for me?" Chloe whispered.

"Yes. I would." *I will no longer be a victim.*

For the first time since the beginning of their conversation, Tasha caught a glimpse of the young girl she'd known as tremulous hope replaced the hardened expression on Chloe's face. "I don't know where to start," Chloe admitted. "And I don't want to hurt her, but it's going to hurt, anyway, when she finds out she was married to a monster."

"Write her a letter," Tasha said, remembering a long-ago conversation with Chloe, who had once professed wanting to be a novelist. "Tap your gift, Chloe. Write her a letter that will make her listen. You can do it. I know you can."

"Why do you care?"

Tasha's tears blurred her vision. "Because we're one in the same and I know how it feels to walk alone."

"Thank you," Chloe whispered, and went into Tasha's arms. "Thank you for believing me."

Tasha blinked back tears and whispered her gratitude to Josh. Without him, she never would've had the strength to offer Chloe anything but her silence. For that and so much more, she'd love him until the day she died—even if they were miles apart.

LATER THAT DAY, JOSH invited Tasha to lunch at a restaurant and she readily accepted, eager to hear an update on Christopher and happy to spend what little time they had left together.

Josh's genuine smile warmed her heart, and as she accepted a modest kiss on her cheek, she tried not to lean into him like a starving woman.

Choosing a quiet spot in the back of the restaurant, Josh pulled out her chair, making her feel cherished and loved. Such a small gesture, she mused, but it definitely worked.

"What's the word on Christopher?" she asked.

"He's on home study for the time being. He and I thought it was best to lie low until his court date. It's only a few days, but I feel better knowing he's home. Plus, since all his computers were confiscated, I know he's not on the Internet."

"You don't think he's learned his lesson?"

"I don't know. I hope so, but I'm glad temptation is no longer within easy reach."

She nodded. "How's things with Carrie?" she asked, concern outweighing her decision to steer clear of that subject.

He sighed heavily. "Not so good. She wants her boyfriend Robert to pull some strings so Christopher can walk away from this scot-free."

Tasha weighed her answer. She knew how Josh

would react to such an offer. Integrity coursed through his veins. But there was some merit to letting Christopher off easy provided he'd learned his lesson as she hoped. She'd hate to see Christopher go into his adulthood with this experience hanging around his neck. "What did you tell her?"

"I told her no."

She decided to put a thought out there. "What if Christopher has already been scared straight, so to speak? Does he really need to have a formal sentence? It seems pretty harsh for a kid his age."

"He broke the law and there are consequences. That's a life lesson he needs to learn," Josh said, though his furrowed brow told her he was struggling with that decision. "He has to take his chances, just like everyone else."

He was right. Tasha admired his stoicism even in the face of his child spending time in juvenile detention. Admiration shone in her smile. "Someday he's going to realize what a good man you are to make this hard choice," she said. "He'll be a better person for it."

He graced her with a smile that melted her heart until she shook off the warm feelings with great effort—especially when she began to wonder what sharing parenting duties with Josh might've been like.

It was too easy to picture a loving home built on the foundation of strong morals and solid ethics; one that overflowed with family energy and echoed with the giggle and chatter of their children. She inhaled sharply as yearning twisted through her, and she looked away for fear he'd see straight into her private thoughts.

"Tasha...I've never been good at poetry. Hell, I can barely write a letter worth reading, but when I look at you, I see everything that's beautiful in the world."

Tears gathered behind her eyes. She felt the same when she looked at him. "No fair," she said, trying for levity, knowing she had to be strong for the both of them. "You say things like that and I'll be tempted to put you in my bag when I leave."

The light in his gaze dimmed as the full impact of what she'd said sunk in. She was leaving. Nothing had changed. His smile faded and she was sorry to see it go. It was probably the most beautiful smile she'd ever seen. "You're still leaving?"

Tasha nodded, but it felt wrong. "Josh...I want to stay. Desperately. But what if it doesn't work out? What if what we had in the past was so much better in our memories than what we could create in the future? I'm not willing to risk it."

"If you're leaving, do it for the right reasons, Tasha."

Dumbfounded, she just stared. He continued quietly, "My feelings for you are unfathomable. Just when I think I've tapped the bottom of the well, you show up and I realize they go so much deeper. Touching you is like knowing a small piece of heaven. Being with you feels as it should've been years ago. We've lost so much time already, I don't want to waste another minute. My life started again the day of your mother's funeral. The past was great, but I know our future is better."

Emotion best left unnamed flooded through her body, crying out to accept everything he was offering, but as she found herself leaning toward the promised land she saw in his blue eyes, fear snaked its way into her heart.

What kind of partnership could she offer Josh? Was it right for him to suffer through the nights when she awoke screaming, clawing at nothing but the bedsheets tangled around her body? He didn't know what he was getting himself into and she could never burden him. Selfishly, she'd give anything to have Josh at her side, to have his strong arms wrapped around her during the night warding off the nightmares with his touch but it wasn't fair. She was broken inside and she was afraid not even his love could put her back together again. She avoided his intense stare and changed the subject.

"I talked to Chloe," she said. "I was right."

Josh grimaced, disgust in his features. "What a bastard. What now?"

"She's going to write her mom a letter, tell her what happened. I think they might have a chance if Diane believes her. Chloe needs to stop running."

"What about you?"

Tasha's fingers stilled on her napkin. "What do you mean?"

"What will it take to get you to stop running?"

She wished she knew the answer. Josh was offering her his heart on a platter. What if she broke it because she couldn't deal with the past? She wouldn't take that chance. He deserved so much better than what she could give.

"I don't know." Her flat tone reflected nothing of the wailing in her heart and betrayed little of the turmoil churning her stomach. "But it's not fair to expect you to wait and find out. I won't do that to you or Christopher."

"Tasha, I'd wait forever if I thought you'd be there at the end."

She regarded him sadly. "I know—that's why I'd never ask. It's not fair."

"Tasha…"

"No, Josh." Hands shaking, she rose from the table and ran from the restaurant.

CHAPTER TWENTY

TASHA WALKED INTO HER father's home and tried not to give the sorrow tugging at her consciousness more power than it already possessed. Hard choices were called that for a reason. She wasn't a naive girl anymore who believed in happy endings. Leaving was the best course of action for the sake of her sanity. Her heart would just have to adjust.

Gerald appeared from his hobby room, a satisfied smile on his face. Even though Josh had finished the room a week or so ago, Gerald had yet to take a look. Tasha suspected he was gathering the courage to face it, knowing somehow that hole represented something else in his mind. She returned his smile.

"That's some good work. Can't hardly tell it was busted through," he said as she came to stand beside him. Everything still needed to be put back in its place, but the fresh paint and new window gleamed. "Josh did a great job."

"Yes, he did. Christopher helped a bit, too," she added, not wanting to leave Chris out even though his contribution had been minimal. "You ought to consider Josh and his brothers in the spring for the back porch. There's a spot where the wood feels soft."

Gerald acknowledged her with a slow, contemplative nod. "I might do that. I was thinking of tearing it down and starting fresh, but just never got around to it. But you're right. Come spring, it might be unsafe. Your mom used to love to watch the sunset from the back porch."

"I remember," Tasha said, leaning against the door frame. "It was her favorite time of the day."

"That it was," he agreed.

"So, you feeling okay? I'm surprised Natalie has allowed you to get out of bed," Tasha said, putting off what she really came to do.

"I don't feel like hauling wood anytime soon, but other than that, my ticker feels fine. How about you? You seem a little off. Something between you and Josh?"

"Dad, we're just friends."

He grunted. "Then you're a damn fool."

"Excuse me?"

"You heard me."

"For someone who just kissed death, you're not very appreciative of your loved ones," Tasha remarked wryly.

"Yeah, well, I made a promise and I aim to say what needs to be said, and I'm not going to pretty it up to get my point across."

"Dad, no one would ever accuse you of 'prettying things up.'"

"True enough. But you and Josh…that kind of thing doesn't come along often. You ought to grab it and hold on for dear life. He's a good man. You could do a lot worse."

"He's a wonderful man," she readily agreed, yet her heart did a painful stutter as she prepared to utter her next statement. "But I'm returning to Belize and his life is here in Emmett's Mill. That's just how things are."

FOR A LONG MOMENT, Gerald regarded his daughter. The time had come for him to make amends, but his courage was flagging. How does a man apologize for letting his daughter twist in the wind when she needed her father the most? Shame almost kept his mouth shut, but the gentle voice of his wife filtered into his mind and gave him the boost he needed.

"Tasha?"

She watched him curiously. "Yeah, Dad?"

"Can we sit a spell? Talk a little?"

"Isn't that what we're doing?" she asked, uncertainty in her green eyes. When he gestured for her to follow him into the living room, she did, but her expression had become concerned.

"What's on your mind?" she asked, taking a seat on the sofa. He chose to sit beside her rather than his lounge chair. She frowned. "Are you okay?"

He waved away her question, anxious to get to the point. "I know you have your reasons for leaving, but I want you to hear me out and then make your decision." She started to protest, but he gently grasped her hand and held it, the action in itself startling enough to snap her mouth shut and stare with wide-eyed worry. He was acting out of character, but maybe this whole time he'd been acting wrong. He drew a deep breath. "I let you down and I was too proud to admit it all these years. I can't take back the past and I can't do what I should've done then, but I can do what I think is right now."

"Dad, you don't have to do this," she said, but the quiet pain in her eyes said differently. "The past is the past. Let's leave it at that."

"Not yet," he said resolutely. "I mean to make amends and you're going to let me. I wronged you, girl. My oldest daughter." His voice cracked. "My pride and joy. I wish I could go back in time and do a lot of things over. I hate myself for not being the man I should've been for you. Your mama tried— bless her heart—to get me to talk to you, but my stubborn pride kept me from doing what was right. I should've killed him," he said in a low voice, wishing Bronson Lewis was alive again just so he could have the pleasure of putting him back in the ground. Tears filled her eyes and his lower lip trembled at the sight. "I don't want to see you running from a good man and the chance of a good life because of that sorry SOB and my cowardice. You deserve so much more."

"Daddy…" She choked on the word and he squeezed her hand, knowing he was a poor substitute for the warmth of her mother. "You don't know what it means to me to hear you say that."

"I have an idea," he said. "When I think of how it would've felt to live without your mama all those years I damn near can't stand the thought. Feels a lot like it does now. And I think you're selling your future short with Josh if you leave."

"I wish it were that simple," she whispered. "I

can't stand the thought of running into Diane all the time. This town's too small. It hurts too much."

Gerald sighed deeply. "That's not something you're going to have to worry about. Diane is moving. She came by the other day to tell me a few things. Felt she needed to get it off her chest." He shook his head sorrowfully. "She said this town's got too many memories that she can't trust."

"What do you mean?" Tasha asked, confused.

"Seems she got a letter from Chloe. Apparently, Bronson hurt his own daughter, too."

A wild surge of respect made Tasha inhale sharply, but she bit her lip against any words she might've said. *Good job, Chloe.* God only knew how hard it must have been to sit down and pen that letter. If only Tasha had been as brave.

"I'm disgusted I once considered him a friend. He was rotten to the core. If there's a hell, hopefully he's roasting in it."

A slow smile crept onto her lips and Gerald knew she was hoping the same thing. Like father, like daughter. Gerald regarded his daughter with open affection. She was his girl and always would be. "I miss you, Tasha."

Her eyes watered and suddenly she launched into his arms. "Daddy, I miss you, too."

Gerald closed his eyes and saw Missy smiling. He

sent a prayer to heaven thanking God for a second chance at making things right.

TASHA PULLED AWAY, almost giddy at the light feeling in her heart. She hadn't realized how much it would mean to her to hear those words from her father, but now that she had, it carried significant weight.

"I'm glad Diane believed Chloe," she said, and he winced.

"Yeah, me, too. It's what I should've done."

She swallowed. "You believe me now. That's what matters."

"You have your mama's heart," he said. "I don't deserve your forgiveness, but I'll take it just the same."

She nodded. "What's going to happen with Chloe?"

Gerald drew a heavy sigh. "I don't know. She's pretty messed up from what Diane's told me. Drugs, petty theft, some prostitution. That girl's got a long road ahead of her."

"Where will they go?"

"She didn't say, but I suspect somewhere far from here where they can get a fresh start."

"I can barely fathom how Chloe must've coped with such an awful secret. I know how I felt, but it was probably a tenth of what she went through."

Gerald nodded, loathing still etched on his weathered face. "I can't believe I let that man sit at my dinner table," he said.

"Did Mom ever know?" Tasha asked.

"About what Bronson did to you?"

She swallowed and nodded.

"No. I never told her, but she was a smart woman. I think she pieced together the puzzle eventually. I couldn't bring myself to talk about it. When she realized what must've happened, she stopped talking to Diane."

Tasha inhaled sharply. It was amazing how one person could shatter so many lives. As she gazed at her father's face, loving every weathered detail, she wondered how a man like her father found and fell in love with someone like her mother.

"When did you know you were in love with Mom?" she asked.

He seemed taken aback by her question and answered slowly at first, then warmed to the memory. "She was always the prettiest thing I ever did see. Turned more than my head in her day, but she didn't think much of me when we first met. But your mother had a gentle soul, one that knew how to calm the hothead in me. And she could dance! Boy, could she dance. When we danced, she made me feel like Fred Astaire." His eyes shone with an inner light as he reminisced. Gaze clearing, he said, "Once I'd won her heart your mama always made me feel like I was the best in the world."

Tasha's eyes watered. "That's so sweet, Dad."

Gerald's cheeks reddened a little but he nodded. "I was lucky to have a woman like your mama for as long as I did." He gave her a long stare. "And you're lucky to have Josh. He was a good boy and he's turned into a fine man."

"You used to terrorize him when we were kids," she teased.

"Of course I did. But he didn't scare easily. I like that in a person. Shows strong character. And, Tasha, I wanted you to expect the best in whomever you gave your heart to, because you're worth it. All my girls are."

Tasha could only stare. She had no idea the depth of her father's love until this moment. She also caught the magnitude of his shame for not being the man she needed him to be so many years ago.

A long moment passed between them as Tasha digested everything her father had just told her and her own reaction to it, when he drew himself up with a deep breath and pinned her with that uncompromising stare he'd perfected when she was a teenager. "So, are you staying this time for good or are you heading back to the jungle?"

CHAPTER TWENTY-ONE

JOSH AND CHRISTOPHER WERE heading into the courthouse for Christopher's hearing when Carrie and
Robert arrived. Josh told Chris to go ahead inside and
then met Carrie at the steps.

"Where's Tasha?" Carrie asked, her tone sarcas-
tic. "I figured she'd be here."

"Only immediate family or guardians are allowed
into the juvenile court proceedings." He looked pointedly at Robert, who shrugged and indicated he'd
wait in the car. "But if it weren't for that rule, I'd have
invited her."

Carrie's mouth looked pinched. "I guess my feelings don't matter anymore."

Josh knew she was talking from a place of hurt
feelings that stemmed from their earlier years and
chose to gentle his words in deference to the love
they once shared. "We aren't married anymore,

Carrie. You've moved on and I have, too. We can go to court if you like, but Christopher is old enough to decide who he wants to live with. He's already made his decision."

Carrie's expression faltered and for a split second he almost felt bad for her. "We don't need to fight. Chris loves you, but he's not crazy about Robert."

"And he just loves Tasha, doesn't he? Everyone does," she added under her breath.

"Please stop, Carrie," he said. "You're going to have to get over this problem you have with Tasha, because I love her and I'm not going to let her go without a fight. That's a promise. We're here for Christopher today. Let's not lose sight of that. Our personal lives are simply that…personal."

Carrie stared. A small amount of moisture gathered at the corners of her eyes. "It's really over between us."

He nodded. "It has been for a long time."

She swallowed. "But it was good while it lasted, right?"

He gave her a smile. "You gave me my son. For that, I will always care for you."

She accepted that and gestured toward the courthouse. "We better get in there. The hearing starts in five minutes."

Josh agreed but had one final thing to say. "Thank you, Carrie."

She gave him a grudging look, but it was sincere. "If you love her, she's the luckiest woman in the world. You're a good man. I wish it had been different for us."

Josh felt a shift between them. The animosity dissipated and Josh knew they could be civil in the future. He breathed a sigh of relief. He didn't want to fight anymore. He had better things to do.

Such as convince Tasha to stay and marry him.

TASHA SAT WITH NATALIE at the bookstore, holding Colton while Natalie closed down the register for the day.

"He's so beautiful, Nat. You've really outdone yourself on this kid."

"Hopefully, we didn't spend all our good genes."

"I don't know, Nat…he's pretty special," Tasha joked, enjoying the feel of his soft body cuddled against her. She pressed a kiss to his downy head. "Look at all that blond curly hair. He must get that from Evan."

Natalie nodded. "Maybe our next one will have at least my hair or eyes. Sometimes it feels like I'm tucking a miniature Evan into bed each night, they're so much alike."

Tasha leaned back to take a better look at Colton. "He looks like you, too. He's got your stubborn cowlick in the front. Although, that's a rather dubious inheritance," she teased, then latched on to something. "Why all this talk about another one? Are you guys thinking of adding to the family?"

Natalie paused and Tasha stared at her. "Nat? What's going on? Are you okay? You look a little green."

"I didn't want to say anything…"

"Are you pregnant?" Tasha asked with growing excitement. Natalie nodded slowly and Tasha wanted to jump up and squeeze her tight, but Colton was asleep in her arms. "That's fantastic! Why haven't you said anything?" Then another thought came to her. "No wonder you've been so exhausted. And what were you thinking taking on so much work? For crying out loud, you should've said something."

"I know, but the timing was terrible. I found out a week before Mom died and it didn't seem right to be celebrating when we were surrounded by so much tragedy. I'm just about three months."

Natalie's eyes watered and Tasha gently laid Colton in his portable crib so she could go to her. She could imagine Natalie's conflicted feelings and felt like a toad for being so selfish. "I wish I'd known…I would've been more…"

"Helpful, considerate, less of a pain in my ass?"

Tasha grinned. "Yeah."

Natalie shrugged. "Don't worry. You had your own stuff to go through. How are you doing?"

"I'm doing good. Dad and I had a long talk. You were right. I needed to talk to him about it. I didn't realize what a difference it would make. I feel…good."

"I'm glad. What about Nora? Have you talked to her yet?"

Tasha sighed. "No. But I will. She deserves to know why I've made the decisions I've made. Maybe it'll go a little way toward mending our relationship. You know, you said she didn't know me, but we don't really know each other. I caught a glimpse of her at the hospital and I have to tell you, she's a kick in the pants."

"You have no idea," Natalie said dryly. "She's also pushy, bossy and nosy, so be careful what you wish for. But she's also loyal, generous and the best person to have in your corner."

"Sounds like Dad."

"Like peas in a pod. But I wouldn't recommend telling her that. She's a little testy about it."

"Good to know."

Tasha's gaze strayed to Natalie's belly and she noted the subtle swelling. She didn't know how that had escaped her notice. It just went to show how self-absorbed she'd been. She'd completely missed Natalie's pregnancy with Colton and she hated the idea of missing out on the birth of her next niece or nephew. Her father's wisdom echoed in her mind and she wondered if her future was here instead of in Belize as she'd thought.

As if reading her turmoil, Natalie asked, "I get the feeling you're getting ready to return to the Peace Corps. I'd hoped you would stay, but if it's not right for you, I can't ask you to go against what your heart is telling you."

That's just it, her heart was telling her—no, screaming—for her to stay, but she didn't know what the right decision was. It seemed ridiculously naive to hope she and Josh could just pick up where they left off and live happily ever after. They weren't the same people anymore.

Natalie broke into her thoughts. "I'm the one who thinks everything through, but I learned sometimes you have to listen to your heart and not your head, because your head has baggage that your heart doesn't carry. If you love Josh, then stay and take a chance. There's a world of wonderful just waiting for you if you're brave enough to take that leap."

"When did you become so wise?" she joked from the curtain of her gathering tears.

"When I had to become the big sister for a while."

Tasha choked up and they embraced. Natalie whispered into her ear, "Come back to us, Tasha. Your home is here."

Was it possible to write over the bad memories with new ones? Tasha thought of her sisters and the new baby Natalie carried. She thought of her father and their new beginning. And lastly, she thought of Josh. Softening, she pulled away from Natalie and knew what she was feeling was written on her face. She wanted, she *craved,* a life with that man. For so long, she'd been terrified of him finding out, knowing what had happened to her, but he knew and it hadn't scared him away. His reaction wasn't what she'd imagined it would be. And although countless counselors had already tried to tell her, it didn't quite sink in until this very moment. It wasn't her fault. She'd done nothing wrong.

But life-changing moments were frightening,

even when they offered good things to come. Natalie read the fear and smiled.

"You deserve a good life. A life with a good man. I think we both know who that man is. Don't let life pass you by because you were too afraid to grab it."

Tasha nodded slowly. "I won't."

"YOUNG MAN, DO YOU understand the seriousness of the charges leveled against you?"

The judge, a forbidding older woman with sharp, dark eyes, peered at Christopher with judgment in her expression.

"Yes, Your Honor," Christopher answered with only the slightest wobble to his voice.

"It distresses me to see so many young kids today with a total disregard for the property of others simply because they want to do something. It comes down to a lack of good parenting, in my opinion," she grumbled, sending a pointed look at both his parents. Christopher was ashamed that the judge was making assumptions on his father because of his own actions. "Do you have anything to say in your defense?"

"There's nothing I can say that will make what I did better. I didn't realize how serious it was, but I do now and I feel bad for the embarrassment this has caused my family." He swallowed and looked to his mom and dad, who were watching him with soft expressions. "I promise I won't do anything like this again."

The judge regarded him with a hard stare and Christopher was tempted to fidget under the assessing gaze, but he sensed she was sizing him up, and if there was one thing he'd learned from his grandfather it was that Halvorsens hold their heads up even under adversity. Finally, she dropped her focus to the paperwork before her. "I believe you. Unfortunately, you've broken the law and therefore there are consequences."

Christopher's knees weakened and he gulped audibly as he waited for his sentence. The tension built in the room as the judge took her sweet time until Christopher was sure he might pass out from the air trapped in his lungs.

Unexpectantly, the judge's thin lips lifted and fell in a smile so subtle Christopher was almost unsure he'd even seen it. "Fortunately for you Zodiac Games has dropped the charges contingent on your promise to turn that genius brain of yours into something useful. Seeing as your intent was selfish rather than malicious, they see no point in throwing you in jail. You've been given a second chance, kid. Don't blow it. If I see you in my courtroom again, you will not find mercy. Do you hear me?"

"Loud and clear," he said gratefully, still reeling from the realization he wasn't going to jail. "Thank you. You won't regret this."

"Mmm. See that I don't." The judge rapped the gavel. "Case closed."

Christopher turned to his parents and they both took turns wrapping their arms around him. A weight dropped from his shoulders, and if he could fly, he certainly would've shot into the sky.

He made a promise to himself never to put his family in this kind of position again. The rewards weren't worth the price it cost, he realized. He hoped Og had learned a similar lesson, though somehow he doubted Og would appreciate Zodiac's leniency. Christopher also realized that his friendship with Og was over. It was a full minute before Christopher recognized cutting off ties to Og was probably a blessing. He doubted they were headed down the same path.

"We have to go, son," Carrie said, gesturing to Robert to wait when he motioned impatiently. "But we're still on for next weekend, right?"

He nodded, but he didn't put much faith in her

showing up, although he was glad she came today. "Sure, Mom."

She must've heard the lack of faith in his voice, for she drew him in another hug. "Just you and me, kid. No Robert. Wherever you want to go and whatever you want to do…provided it doesn't involve computers."

He grinned. "No golf lessons?"

"Golf? The only good thing about golf is being able to drive the cart. No golf lessons. I promise."

"Thanks, Mom."

"No problem, son." She looked at Josh and nodded softly as they communicated something he wasn't privy to. He didn't need to know, he could feel the difference between them. It was about time.

CHAPTER TWENTY-TWO

TASHA WAS IN HER HOTEL room sitting on the bed with her laptop open when there was an urgent knock at her door. She'd only just e-mailed her director to tell him her decision and she was still a little over-whelmed, but she knew it was the right one.

Rising, she padded to the door and peered into the peephole.

Josh stood in the hallway, his expression unusually tense. Immediately concerned for the results of Christopher's court hearing, she opened the door with a question ready when Josh pulled her into his arms so that he could plant a soul-searing kiss on her mouth.

Happily drowning in the sensations of being devoured, Tasha ceased to remember that she'd had any other concerns. Slowly pulling away, Josh cradled her body as if it were the rarest treasure and looked deep into her eyes. "Tasha, it doesn't make sense. It defies logic, but you're a part of me and I can't let you go without putting up a fight."

The desire he'd whipped up with the force of his kiss ebbed, but in its place was something heartier that she couldn't put into words. Her stunned silence gave Josh the wrong impression and he started in earnest.

"I love you, Tasha. I want what we couldn't have the day we walked away from each other. I want to spend the rest of my life making up for that one moment. If you feel the same way, please give us a chance to find out what our future holds." He drew her even closer until their noses almost touched, their breath mingling as one. "I want to see our child with your eyes. And I don't want to wait another minute to have you permanently by my side. If you're scared I'll hold your hand. If you have bad dreams I'll chase them away, and if you need a shoulder mine is and always has been yours. Please say yes. Make me the happiest man in the world. Say…yes."

Tears blinded her, but her head bobbed in a nonsensical manner that almost qualified as hysterical. It was a dream come true in a past filled with nightmares. She saw stars and felt drunk, although she hadn't touched a drop of liquor in years. She latched on to his mouth like a woman drowning and answered between fervent kisses that took her breath away.

"Yes! Forever yes!"

Within that moment the last remaining timber of the wall she'd constructed around herself splintered and cracked, falling away to reveal the fast-beating heart of a woman with an incredible capacity to love and be loved.

And Tasha wasn't wasting another minute. She was terribly behind and they had a lot of catching up to do.

"I want a handful of sons and an equal number of daughters, Josh Halvorsen," she said against his mouth, pulling at his shirt and jerking at the button on his jeans. "Starting…right now!"

They tumbled onto the bed and Tasha—nipping, kissing and savoring—showed him just how serious she was. By the satisfied grin on Josh's face, he didn't seem to mind one bit—which was a good thing because there was a whole lot more where that came from.

Something along the lines of a lifetime supply.

* * * * *

Be sure to read Nora's story,
A KISS TO REMEMBER (SR #1487),
coming in April 2008
wherever Harlequin Books are sold!

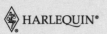

Romantic
SUSPENSE

Sparked by Danger,
Fueled by Passion.

When Tech Sergeant Jacob "Mako" Stone opens
his door to a mysterious woman without a past,
he knows his time off is over. As threats to Dee's
life bring her and Jacob together, she must set
aside her pride and accept the help of the military
hero with too many secrets of his own.

Out of Uniform
by Catherine Mann

Available February wherever you buy books.

HARLEQUIN®

Mediterranean NIGHTS™

Sometimes you need someone to teach you the things you already know....

Coming in February 2008

CABIN FEVER

by

Mary Leo

Vacationing aboard *Alexandra's Dream* with her two kids and her demanding mother-in-law, widow Becky Montgomery is not about to start exploring love again. But when she meets Dylan Langstaff, the ship's diving instructor, she realizes she might be ready to take the plunge....

Available wherever books are sold starting the second week of February.

HARLEQUIN
Super Romance

COMING NEXT MONTH